Paula Jane Rodgers was born in 1971 in Huddersfield, West Yorkshire. She attended the local schools and college there. Taking time out from working in an office she became a housewife and during this period she wrote down her dreams and ideas, accomplishing one of her life ambitions in the form of her first novel.

CURATOR ANGELUS

Paula Jane Rodgers

CURATOR ANGELUS

Vanguard Press

VANGUARD PAPERBACK

© Copyright 2017
Paula Jane Rodgers

The right of Paula Jane Rodgers to be identified as author of
this work has been asserted by her in accordance with the
Copyright, Designs and Patents Act 1988.

A CIP catalogue record for this title is
available from the British Library.

This is a work of fiction. Names, characters, businesses, places, events and incidents are
either the products of the author's imagination or used in a fictitious manner. Any
resemblance to actual persons, living or dead, or actual events is purely coincidental.

ISBN 978 1 784652 22 7

Vanguard Press is an imprint of
Pegasus Elliot MacKenzie Publishers Ltd.
www.pegasuspublishers.com

First Published in 2017

Vanguard Press

Sheraton House Castle Park
Cambridge England
Printed & Bound in Great Britain

To my husband, Richard, and my son, Corey, for their continued
support throughout the writing of this book.

Chapter One

The Waterfall

Victoria Willis, or Vicky as she was known to her family and close friends, was in an upright position inside the flow of the waterfall, levitating above the river. Her vulnerable soul was showing fear through her beautiful big blue eyes. The waterfall's almighty pressure and her sheer exhaustion made it impossible for her to keep her head up. With her slim arms forced straight out to the sides and her legs limply dangling beneath her, Vicky's thin body was totally defenceless. An almost silent screech, quieter than a mouse, was all she could manage when she attempted to scream.

The natural elements of nature were no match for the powerful invisible entity that had total control over her. Murky water relentlessly poured through Vicky's blonde hair and over her flawless skin. Finding it increasingly harder to breathe she took deep intakes of air whenever possible, coughing and spluttering as she tried not to swallow the dirty water. Her pretty, red flowery dress clung to her. Goosebumps covered every part of her body whilst at the same time her teeth began to chatter. Deep purple bruising had started to appear almost instantly around her wrists and throat. Her face only became visible when her hair was pulled upwards. Deep bite marks appeared on her face and neck as the water instantly rinsed away the blood.

Vicky had long since closed her eyes, putting herself somewhere else until eventually losing consciousness. Eventually gravity taking hold and allowing her pale lifeless body to fall heavily straight down into the river, hitting the water below with a thud, making it sound like she had hit a concrete surface. The entity had finished with her, it had had its fun.

Ben Cooper and Amanda Styles, who were Vicky's closest friends, had already deserted her only moments earlier. They had fled the scene screaming, whilst the Ouija board floated down the river, bobbing up and down with the flow. Vicky had been sat around that very same board without a care in the world, with her so-called friends, only a little while earlier.

Lisa Parkins, a timid girl, had heard the laughter when she was walking alone along the woodland path on her way home from her nature walk one late afternoon. Catching sight of the group of friends and not wanting them to see her she hid a short distance away from them, curious to see what they were doing. Being careful not to hurt herself she sat on an old fallen tree trunk which was covered in green moss and partially hidden behind an overgrown holly bush. Once in position and keeping herself balanced she managed to watch them through a small gap between some of the branches and was still clearly able to hear their conversations. Lisa could see Beechwood Park just a stone's throw away, at the other side of the river.

They were all older than Lisa. Leaving school the year before, she believed them to be college students. Remembering that they always hung around school together, Ben had always been Lisa's schoolgirl crush, hers and probably half of the girls at school at some point. In return he had never even noticed her, he was too busy being in love with himself, admiring his Mediterranean good looks in his reflection at every given opportunity.

Amanda was Ben's dippy on-off girlfriend, an average looking girl who was a bubbly brunette who wore spectacles.

Ben could no longer contain his excitement as he opened up the old box that contained the Ouija board. It was a plain old brown tatty box, which had more than its fair share of dust on. Once inside the box he treated it as though it were the crown jewels, carefully placing it and the glass message indicator onto an already flattened patch of grassed area. They had planned to make a day of it, taking along a picnic, which they had set up on the blanket next to them. Vicky's contribution was a selection of homemade sandwiches which she had lovingly prepared that morning, raiding the refrigerator at home of any leftover cooked meats and salad. Ben only remembering at the last minute, buying some spicy flavoured crisps and chocolate biscuits from the corner shop on the way down there. Whilst Amanda, who had put no thought into it whatsoever, was more than happy with the variety of cans of fizzy pop she had chosen from the bargain basket in the local supermarket.

Leaving the picnic to one side they all sat down on the grass around the Ouija board and held hands.

"Woooooo." Ben's voice revealing a hint of sarcasm.

Vicky gave out a little laugh, managing to easily stop herself a long time before Amanda and Ben had calmed themselves down, tears streaming down their cheeks.

Vicky waited until they were more rational, looking at them both in turn she tried to put on a sophisticated voice. "Right, you two, shall we try to communicate with a few real spirits now?"

Ben answered before Vicky had time to finish her question. He did not need to be asked twice. "Is anybody there?" He rolled his eyes back to show the whites of his eyes, his pupils and irises disappearing for a short time. "Wooooo. I said, is anybody there?"

Ben once again started to immediately laugh at his own foolishness. He looked over at Amanda and she copied his lead.

"Why do you have to act so stupid all of the time? And why is your hand so hot and sticky, Ben?" Vicky switched her voice to sound more like that of an impatient disgusted school teacher with a facial expression to match.

"I really don't think you want me to answer that one." Ben's cheeky eyes twinkled, his eyebrows rhythmically went up and down whilst he smirked and flared his nostrils. He always found it hard to resist the urge to wind Vicky up at any given opportunity.

"Urgh. Ben, you are a disgusting creature. Behave yourself and pack it in." Vicky tried her best to be serious and once again succeeded after almost giving into a smile.

"Let me have a try." Amanda let go of Ben and Vicky's hands, stretched out her arms in front of her and wiggled her fingers. Looking skywards and closing her eyes she continued. "You are now in my power... I am calling out to the dark side... Is there anybody there who would like to communicate with us?"

Vicky tutted out loud, her patience was wafer thin at the best of times and she was even more irritable than her usual charming self. "We're supposed to hold the glass on the board for it to work, stupid people. I've seen it done loads of times in the movies. I'm practically an expert you know."

"You're that all right." Ben sat there waiting for Vicky to make some sort of response. He was bursting at the seams to wind Vicky up some more.

He was not left disappointed. "Go on, Ben, spit it out. I know you're dying to try and say something really witty."

"I just wanted to say that you're that all right."

"What?"

"An egg spurt."

Vicky pushed Ben on the top of his arm, causing him to lose his balance slightly. Using this as an excuse Ben and Amanda rolled about in the grass together in fits of laughter, squashing any daisies that had not already been flattened, whilst Vicky sat there shaking her head and doing her not amused impression.

Looking down at her watch Lisa could not believe how long she had been sat there. Standing up to make her way home, she was stopped in her tracks when she heard a high pitched squeal coming from the direction of the group. Checking to make sure that they had not seen her she slowly sat back down again. Staying as still and quiet as she could, she carefully moved up closer to the bush to try to get a better look.

Amanda continued to make random high pitched squealing noises whilst pointing at the board frantically. "Look it moved. The glass moved by itself. It's moved and is pointing towards the *Yes*. Look." Getting slightly out of control she stood up and started to jump up and down.

"Okay, calm down, Amanda. There's no need to get all hysterical. It's probably on a bit of a slope and has just slid down, coincidentally landing on the Yes. It can't just move by itself." Vicky turned to look at Ben suspiciously. "Or is it you, Ben? Are you pranking us? What have you done to it? Is it magnetised or something?"

Amanda was keen for the others to believe her. "It's not on a slant, I tell you. I saw it move."

"I haven't done anything to it, I swear." Ben's seriousness already had Vicky convinced.

"Where did you get the board from?" Vicky said curiously, her voice seeming calmer and more caring.

"I found it in that junk shop in the village. You know the one I mean, the one next door to the tobacconist. It was covered in dust and hidden away behind some other old board games. When I asked the old man in the shop how much it was he just said that I could have it. He never even looked up from the book that he was reading. He did say it had been in his shop for years and he just wanted to get rid of it, so he let me have it, for free." Ben's stomach started to make strange growling noises.

"Okay. Let's all just chill out a bit and have something to eat. We'll just have our picnic, pack everything away and we'll go to the pictures or go and do something else instead." Vicky smiled at them both comfortingly.

Amanda and Ben both nodded their heads simultaneously in response. The silliness and laughter had been replaced by a more sombre feel, even when Ben let out a huge accidental burp after drinking too much fizzy pop in one go. Leaving the board and its glass on the grass to one side they sat on the picnic blanket and shared out the food between them. Nothing was said whilst they were eating, instead they all kept looking over towards the board and in turn at each other. The only noises that could be heard were the grinding motions of sandwiches being chewed, the crunching of crisps and biscuits and the slurping of pop.

Sitting there for a good while longer after they had finished eating, none of them really wanting to leave, transfixed by what they had started.

Amanda looked over at Ben. "Go on, I dare you to ask it another question."

"No way, you ask it."

"I thought we were going to pack everything away once we had eaten and go and do something else," Vicky interrupted, appearing quite concerned whilst trying to convince the other two that it was time to leave. Picking up the empty packets and cans she put them into a carrier bag.

"Ben's a chicken. A big fat chicken." Amanda's childishness shining through.

"What and I suppose you're not then. Prove it, I dare you to ask it another question." Ben was not pretending any more, he really just wanted to go home.

"Goodness me, give up you two. I'll do it. We do this one more time and then we go. Are we agreed?" Vicky picked up the glass and carefully put it back down in the centre of the board, keeping her hand on it she said, "Who are you? What is your name? To whom do you wish to communicate?"

There was no response, the glass did not move. Vicky moved her hand away from it. Turning to the other two she said, "See nothing, now let's just go and do something else instead. This is getting really boring now."

Amanda and Ben continued staring at the board. Vicky rolled her eyes, tutted and sighed, in that order and tried again. She asked the same questions and got the same response, nothing. Sitting perfectly still, only their eyes moved, from side to side, when they looked at each other suspiciously. Even Vicky joined in when they all burst out laughing.

No sooner had they started laughing when the glass randomly moved on its own again, pointing straight to the 'V', without any hesitation. The laughter stopped as they were no longer able to take their eyes away from the board. It did not disappoint them, after a few seconds it slowly glided and pointed to the 'I'. In unison, Amanda and Ben both turned their heads and looked straight at Vicky.

"What?" Vicky said, seemingly unaware.

As the message indicator moved again, this time quicker it pointed at 'C'. They were left with no doubts that it most definitely wanted to communicate with Vicky.

Amanda could no longer take any more, standing up she started to scream and ran away in the direction of her home. Ben followed closely behind her, leaving Vicky sitting there alone.

"It's okay, you two, just leave me to tidy up. You two just run away." Still perfectly calm Vicky stood up and reached down to pick up the board, not giving it the chance to continue to spell out her full name. Throwing the board and the glass straight into the river, the glass smashed against a rock shattering it into little pieces.

"Stupid game anyway," Vicky said out loud to herself, hoping that Ben and Vicky might hear.

Vicky felt a force push her against her chest and stomach, causing her to feel winded. Stumbling and falling backwards, she landed harshly on her backside. She frantically looked around but could not see anything. Rubbing her bottom and grabbing at her chest she took a deep breath. "Ouch that really hurt. I don't know who you are or what you want with me but please just leave me alone."

Getting to her feet again she tried walking towards the path. It was not going to let her go, it had other ideas; instead it had got behind her and dragged her backwards by her hair whilst she reached up and tried to stop the pulling. Momentum picked up as she lost her footings. Big clumps of hair fell onto the ground, leaving a trail behind her along with her shoes as she was dragged down the banking and towards the river. Open sores on her legs were stinging and bleeding from being pulled through the tangled brambles. The unforgiving force continued dragging her through the water until finally it reached the waterfall.

"You did not let me finish my game, Victoria." The entity finally spoke. "I am here to punish you for your inappropriate behaviour and because I have waited more than long enough for my retribution for events long ago." It was a surprisingly gentle but masculine voice, the last voice Vicky would ever hear. This was to be where Vicky would spend the final moments of her life with the invisible entity inflicting vengeance upon her.

Ben and Amanda had reached the end of the towpath, leaving a dust trail behind them whilst managing to scare the local wildlife in the process, with the birds flapping wildly in the treetops and the ducks squawking in the water. Beating any personal best records, they ran in opposite directions to their homes, neither looking nor speaking to the other to check that they were all right.

Opening the front door to his home and not closing it behind him Ben ran straight up the stairs without taking his jacket and trainers off first. Running into his bedroom, he locked the door behind him; closing his curtains, he jumped on top of his bed, dirtying the duvet cover in the process. Laying on his back with his arms out to the sides and legs opened he tried to calm down his heartbeat, feeling the beats palpitating against his ribcage and pulsating in his eardrums. Still wide eyed he stared up to the ceiling, trying to make sense of the shadows.

His mother, Fiona, knocked on his door, interrupting the beat. "Ben, sweetheart. Are you okay?"

Jumping, Ben said, "Yes I'm fine, Mum, I just want to be left alone." Holding up his hands and reaching towards the ceiling, he tried to stop them from shaking. His parents left him alone in his room, allowing him to come out and explain things in his own good time.

Amanda had managed to run all the way home without stopping to catch her breath. Bursting straight into the kitchen she tried to explain to her father, Owen, what had happened with the Ouija board.

Owen pulled out a kitchen chair and patted the seat cushion with the palm of his hand. "Slow down girl. Just sit down and start from the beginning."

Sitting down at the side of Amanda, he sat patiently and waited for her to explain. After several attempts of getting tongue-tied, backtracking and gasping for breath Amanda managed to say everything that she wanted to.

"What have I said to you, Amanda, in the past? God give me strength. Will you never listen? Will you never learn? I have told you numerous times to stay away from anything like that. Ouija boards are extremely dangerous instruments. If you don't understand something then don't mess with it," Owen said with a look of disappointment and a half-smile of reassurance thrown in.

"I am sorry, Dad. We were just having a laugh. We didn't think anything would really happen." Tears turned into black streaks, which ran down Amanda's cheeks and reddened her eyes.

"You say that you and Ben left Vicky by herself. Let's hope nothing bad has happened." Owen smiled trying to reassure her. He tied the laces on his trainers and reached up to the coat hook for his jacket.

As they walked briskly back to where the incident occurred Owen continued lecturing Amanda, telling horror stories about Ouija boards and how someone he had known when they were teenagers had come face to face with the devil at their peril. Amanda as usual, was not listening, she did not want to go back but felt bad for leaving Vicky there.

Arriving too late, Vicky's body had already been discovered in the river, at the base of the waterfall with the water still lashing down on her. Amanda and Owen went to the grassed area where the three of them had been playing. The picnic blanket and the bag of empty packaging were still there with no sign of the Ouija board.

Amanda tried to explain to the police what had happened with the Ouija board but the police did not take her seriously and were only really half-listening to her story. They concluded that after Amanda and Ben had left Vicky by herself, the perpetrator must have decided to make his move. He had more than likely been watching them and waited before attacking her. Vicky would never have stood a chance. They could not find any DNA evidence and blamed that on the fact that she had been in the water and there were no known witnesses.

Vicky's death certificate stated that she had died from asphyxiation. The police were looking for someone or possibly more than one murderer. To this day, the police still have it on record as an unsolved case.

Lisa had witnessed every detail, but still many years later, she could not breathe a word to anybody about what she had seen. It was just something that she would have to take to the grave with her.

Chapter Two

Beechwood Park

Apart from the occasional out-of-the-ordinary incident, Beechwood Park was a mostly peaceful place and was large enough for everyone to have their own space, if they needed it.

During the spring and summer months, the river would flow gently alongside the park and the local wildlife would enjoy its calmness. The waterfall could be heard a short distance away from the river. Daffodils and bluebells grew randomly, wherever they chose, breaking up the dominant greens and browns. Some of the trees would be in full blossom and ready for the seasons ahead. Greens, yellows, blues and pinks would be everywhere that you looked, a splendour of magnificent and beautiful colour.

Autumn was a magical time of year, the remaining leaves on the trees would be numerous shades of reds, browns and gold. Some of the trees would look vulnerable whilst already totally bare. On other trees, the remaining leaves would try to hold on for dear life until a final gust of wind would effortlessly come along and they would be defeated in the blink of an eye and gently fall to the ground. The ground below would be carpeted with these fallen leaves, initially all fresh and crispy until the rains would turn them to mush. Lisa would stroll through them, kicking them into the air and listening to the rustling and crunching noises that were made. Wrapped around her neck and resting on her head would be the multi-coloured chunky knitted scarf and hat that her loving grandmother had made for her a couple of years previous. When late autumn arrived, the wind would change all too quickly, almost overnight, becoming too cold and deviously biting her to the bone.

Lisa had always found the winter months the hardest to cope with. She enjoyed the snow but could not really escape to the park; it was too cold and sometimes even inaccessible. It lost some of its appeal, losing all of its colour, it appeared to be a more dangerous and scary place. The river was a lot deeper and flowed quicker, giving it a more savage and unforgiving appearance. Never flowing clear it was mainly a dirty brown colour from the stirring up of the riverbed, dragging along any broken twigs, branches and leaves along its surface.

Beechwood Park was where Lisa always escaped to when she needed some space from the dramas of her everyday life, which included both her family and school in equal proportions. Lisa hated school but always attended, never playing truant, even going when feeling under the weather.

Her father John had many rules that Lisa had to obey, one being back home before dark. Never wanting to hang around at the park when it was night-time anyway, she never had a problem with that rule. There was very little lighting and the darkness attracted the wrong type of person. The difference in characters that were drawn to the park during the day and night were self-evident.

Lisa was in her own little world as she sat swinging on the old rusty swing, her hands becoming orange stained from the rust of the chains. She would rinse them in the river later before going home. It had only been a couple of weeks previous that she had witnessed the demise of

Victoria Willis. Never being her favourite person, she still felt a little bit raw from the ordeal. Looking across the river towards the waterfall, it all seemed like a distant memory. There was nothing left at the once crime scene to suggest that anything had actually ever happened.

Beechwood was a small village; word had soon got around about Victoria Willis' death. The adults and parents believing that there was a maniac on the loose whilst the younger ones wanted to believe that it was something far more evil and sinister, making up their own theories and version of events. In the evening instead of the adults keeping their children safe indoors they allowed them to go out, only if they stayed in groups and did not wander off by themselves. Most of them would play in the river, some venturing to go near the waterfall and others searched for the Ouija board amongst the brambles and further down the riverbank.

The park was within a short walking distance from where Lisa had been brought up. She had spent many hours playing there by herself, during her childhood and even more so during her teenage years. Her teenage years she found to have been definitely her most difficult. If anybody upset Lisa, which was a regular event, she would escape to the park at the earliest given opportunity. Not having anyone to confide in or comfort her she found that being close to nature had a calming effect on her. Losing track of the time was something that she specialised in, she would be taken away from reality and left to wander into her own daydreams.

Having always been quite a sickly individual she had started to feel nauseous, motion sickness had set in. Braking with her feet, she stopped herself from swinging and concentrated really hard, looking down and staring intensely at her own skinny legs, the nausea soon subsided. Lisa had researched many books over the years including the subject of mind over matter, which was something that she really believed in. Convincing herself that if she wanted something strongly enough then she could make it happen, that included being in control of her own body.

Still sitting on the swing Lisa continued to look down at her badly scuffed shoes and noticed that the soles had managed to break free from the glue once again. John and her mother, Elizabeth, were always first in line at the jumble sales whilst family members passed hand-me-down items onto them too. They were never fashionable or the previous year's fashions either for that matter.

Lisa picked at the stitching on the patch on the knee of her jeans, it had started to come away at the corner and reveal the hole underneath. It would need to be sewn back on again, along with a new patch for the elbow of her sweatshirt.

Jumping from the swing, without a care in the world, Lisa ran over to the old wooden roundabout. Nobody else was about to join her, so whilst holding on tight to the handrail, she kept one foot on the roundabout whilst the other foot hopped up and down on the ground and made it turn. Once spinning Lisa tilted her head back slightly and closed her eyes, smiling when she felt the gentle breeze blow over her face. As her overgrown brown fringe blew upwards she opened her eyes to reveal her translucent blue irises. The roundabout gradually slowed down until it inevitably came to a stop, Lisa jumped off. Try as she might, walking in a straight line was impossible and because Lisa had made herself so dizzy, she fell to the ground. Lying flat on her stomach and lifting her head up, she looked towards the horizon. It appeared to have tilted, moving to a vertical position. Squeezing her eyes shut Lisa grasped hold of two clumps of grass as tightly as she could, to stop herself from sliding into the sky. Only daring to open her eyes a few moments later and feeling relieved when everything had returned back to normality.

Sitting up cross-legged, Lisa looked over to where the slide used to be. The council had been and taken it down a few weeks earlier because it had been a rusty old thing, which had big patches of green leaded paint peeling off. Lisa had entertained herself for hours on that slide. Now in its place was a patch of flattened tarmac where someone had chalked a hopscotch grid.

Running over to the igloo shaped climbing frame, she managed to climb to the top with ease. It was quite high but Lisa showed no fear. Being a keen gymnast and being supple she climbed through the top bars, holding on she dangled her body down inside the frame, allowing her arms to take her body weight. Letting go of the bar Lisa felt herself slowly dropping towards the ground. Pretending to be an Olympic gymnast, she would practice a perfect landing and imitate the cheering of the crowds. She was stopped in her tracks when a strange sensation came over her as she was descending to the ground, it felt like she was falling in slow motion whilst something was holding her firmly around her waist. Not daring to look at who it might be she stared straight ahead and held her breath. Before she landed, just above the ground, she was stopped from making contact. Her entire body became rigid as she stiffened up. The hands gently let her go, where she landed gracefully on both feet. Feeling unnerved she cautiously looked around the park, noting that there was still nobody else about. Climbing quickly back up to the top again, she remained seated, even when the feel of the cold metal had started to penetrate her clothing, making her bottom feel numb.

It had only been a few months previous that Lisa had witnessed Vicky giggling and cavorting in the bushes. Vicky had looked over at Lisa, taunting her by blowing her a kiss before getting it on with her latest conquest. She was quite the exhibitionist. Being quite popular with the boys, it had been rumoured that she had taken many different boys into the bushes, sometimes more than one at a time. She was a very experienced young lady considering she always walked around with her airs and graces. Lisa had only witnessed Vicky on the one occasion and had been sat in that very same place, at the top of the climbing frame. At the time, Lisa's curiosity had managed to get the better of her, so after climbing down she had tip-toed over towards the bush. Not needing to get too close Lisa was able to get a good view, watching Vicky and her companion for a short time, just to confirm if the rumours were true. Both were dressed in the suits that nature had provided, rolling around in the foliage, performing strange sexual acts on each other that Lisa had not known existed until that day.

Getting back to reality, Lisa felt calm again and climbed down carefully this time. Once her feet were on the ground she rubbed her bottom cheeks vigorously so has to relieve the numbness. Walking over to where the skateboarders and BMX riders often played she chuckled to herself as she read some of the graffiti.

If u want sex ring (tel. no.)

YW + BJ 4EVA TGVER 4 YRS TO CUM (heart shape surrounding it and cupid's arrow going through it)

Rick woz ere (month and year stated)

There was the usual oversized drawing of a penis and testicles with sperm splashes squirting from the top. In fact there were several of varying sizes.

Lisa sat down on the bench that was situated right underneath a very old sycamore tree. It sheltered most of the skateboarding area, blocking out any possible sunlight and had been left with a permanent scar on its trunk, a large upside down pentangle had been engraved deeply onto it. Nobody knew who had put it there or why, it had been there for generations. Looking over at the football pitch, Lisa watched with fascination as a couple of pigeons took a long bath in a puddle.

Lisa had wanted to have a go on one of the tree swings but could not find one that was not broken. Some of them had been there for many years and were just pieces of old rope that remained, dangling from the out of reach branches. Instead, she strolled over to sit down at the side of the river.

A middle-aged couple were out walking their dog and rushed past Lisa, giving her a half-hearted smile in return for her warm smile, hurrying about in their own busy worlds and missing out on the real world around them. She did not know or recognise them but thought it polite to give them a smile.

Continuing to watch them Lisa noticed that they had stopped to talk to the lady who owned the local newsagents, Mrs Blake. She was a buxom lady who was nicknamed The Tabloid, on account that she found out about most things before the local newspaper did. Their body language was a giveaway that they were gossiping and laughing about some poor unsuspecting soul.

A group of younger children had arrived and started to play on the swings and roundabout whilst their mothers sat on a bench, occasionally breaking off from their chatter to watch on. Lisa smiled to herself when she saw the children playing, watching them run around, taking it in turn to be 'it' whilst the others jumped over and on everything to get away. They were playing off-ground-tig whilst shouting and pushing each other in a playful manner. Their mothers shouted above the noise of their children, telling them to behave and be careful whilst they paid attention for a couple of minutes and then continued with their antics.

Lisa had blocked out the sound of the children and their mothers and had wandered back into one of her daydreams. Her favourite time of the year had always been the summer, one of the reasons being because the days were longer. She loved to lay in the warmth of the sunshine in the grass on the riverbank, pretending to be someone else who was attractive, had friends and who travelled the world. Faraway places that she had only ever seen on the television and in magazines were her destinations. The bees and butterflies would be going about their business whilst Lisa would stare up at the blue sky and study the shapes of the clouds.

The sky was of particular interest to Lisa. A perfect blue without a cloud or angry and stormy, it did not matter, she still found it beautiful. As she looked up at the sky, a light aircraft flew overhead spoiling her daydream, leaving its white trail behind. Staring at one cloud in particular, she had convinced herself that if she looked at it for long enough she could actually make a hole appear in it.

A squeak from a cheeky fieldmouse broke her concentration. It went up close to Lisa to get a better look but when she held out her hand it scurried away as quickly as it had appeared.

A family of ducks had swum up nearby, one of them was quacking angrily whilst another sounded like it was laughing in response. There were some large stepping-stones laid in the river, which the ducks had perched themselves on. The stones were only really visible in the summer, when the river was low. Lisa had often crossed the river by jumping across them. A larger gap between two of them made it tricky, care was paramount because the stones were mossy in parts, which made them very slippery. Only ever falling in on a couple of occasions was still impressive given that she had crossed them hundreds of times.

Her time had gone all too quickly again, as it always seemed to do when she went to the park. It was time for her to make tracks and head home, Elizabeth would have tea ready for her.

As Lisa started to make tracks a gang of older boys had started to arrive at the park, running past Lisa, shouting obscenities at each other, not really noticing her. The dark haired lanky one who went by the name of Andy could be heard making a clanging noise. The noise was coming from his carrier bag and was quickly followed by the sound of breaking glass. Hurling the bag across the field, he allowed the broken bottles of vodka to lay where they fell, the contents flowing out of the bottle and the bag. They reached the furthest corner of the football field where they hid away amongst the trees.

A stocky fair-haired lad called Adam had been carrying a fire extinguisher underneath his arm. He was the youngest and Andy and Martyn had coaxed him into stealing it from a nearby business, which he had managed to do without any problems.

"What do I do with this syringe?" Martyn was an unfortunate looking character who was underweight and had bad skin. He might as well have been wearing a T-shirt announcing to the world that he was a drug addict. His heroin addiction was taking its toll and slowly ravaging his body, a gentle flow of blood trickling down his forearm, which he cleaned up with his tongue.

"Do you really want me to answer that?" Mike said loudly, looking around at the others for their attention. "Is there anyone here that really gives a shit what Martyn does with it?" Mike was the better looking one of the gang with his dark hair and dark eyes, unfortunately these factors were overpowered by his rudeness and arrogance.

Whilst the rest of the gang were still in fits of laughter, Martyn launched the syringe into a neighbouring field. High as a kite he did not notice the others mocking him, being a pitiful soul he was easily lead.

Trying to impress the others Adam stood up, as though he were on a stage and thought it would be amusing if he started to inhale the contents of the fire extinguisher.

There were chants of encouragement as he put the extinguisher's nozzle to his mouth. "Go' Adam, go' Adam." Within seconds he turned pale, his eyes rolled back has he lost consciousness. Falling forwards, he was not able to put out his hands to save himself. The grass cushioned his fall slightly when he landed on his face. It was not long after that an ambulance arrived at the scene to take Adam to the hospital. The paramedics did not look amused but continued with their jobs professionally without making any comments. He was fortunate that he had only broken his nose and had two lovely matching black eyes. A quick visit to the dentist rectified his broken front tooth problem.

As the nights grew darker, the group had no respect for neighbouring homes, as they got noisier. The surrounding residents complained to each other about the worsening situation.

Frank, an elderly man had noted that they were not even local lads and had seen them arriving on the same number twenty-seven bus, at the same time every night. Frank had been to the local police station to report them but they were not concerned. Their attitude was 'out of sight, out of mind'. At the end of the day, the youngsters had not actually caused anyone any harm and had not caused any criminal damage. Frank was asked to make a record of the dates and the times of any extreme out of the ordinary behaviour, which he was not happy about, he believed this to be a delay tactic.

A few days later Frank had been at the end of his tether with it all and decided that more drastic action would need to be taken. Knowing that the lads were all together he decided that he would walk down and have a little chat with them. Watching from a distance for a short while to ascertain what they were getting up to, he remained calm and in full control of his temper. The years had not been kind to Frank and he was a little frail on his feet, using a stick to aid him with his walking.

The group turned around when they heard Frank walking towards them.

"Evening." Frank was polite but firm, speaking to them as a group, not able to work out who the ringleader was at that stage.

Mike was the obvious spokesperson for the group. "Evening." The others looked at Frank but remained silent.

"Are you lads behaving yourselves tonight?" Frank tried to keep it civil, now only making eye contact with Mike.

"Yeah." Mike looked at Frank as if to say 'Is that it? Run along now.'

Frank had not even started with his interrogation. "What are you lads up to?"

"Oh you know, a little bit of this, a little bit of that." The others started to laugh as they hung on Mike's every word.

"Do you think you can keep the noise down tonight lads? There are a lot of other elderly residents around here. You could take your rubbish home with you too?" Ignoring the laughter Frank felt relieved to be getting it all off his chest and hopeful that it would all get resolved.

Mike turned his back on Frank, focussing his attention back towards the group again, ignoring him; he failed to answer his questions.

"I said, do you think you can keep the noise down? Even better still, how about going back home, there must be somewhere else you lads can hang around." Frank was on a roll, taking him back to the days when he served his time in the Royal Navy, giving out his orders.

Turning his head around and looking over his shoulder Mike looked at Frank like he was something that he had trodden in. "Do us all a favour old man. Go fuck off and just mind your own business."

Frank had not served his time to be spoken to like that. He took his stick and prodded Mike on his back without any warning.

Standing up Mike turned around, pluming his feathers as though he were a peacock he towered over Frank. "What the fuck do you think you are doing old man?"

Remaining calm Frank felt a little intimidated, he carried on. "I'm asking you and your friends to keep the noise down. It's not rocket science, young man, so I'm sure you'll be able to cope with a simple instruction."

Continuing Mike looked down on Frank, with an angry expression, he pointed his index finger in Frank's face. "You've just assaulted me. Lay one more finger on me and I'll have you."

An expression of disbelief appeared on Frank's face. He was now of the understanding that a sensible response would not be given. Speaking louder and slower, he exaggerated his words. "Do you understand the definition of respect? Please answer my question. Are you going to keep the noise down? Apologies let me ask you that question again, in a way that you may understand a little better. Are you going to keep the fucking noise down?"

Mike was both shocked and furious that a little old man had dared to try to humiliate him, especially in front of his friends. Flying at Frank his face was red with anger. Surprisingly Frank's reactions were quicker than Mike had anticipated as he jabbed Mike straight in the stomach with his stick. Stumbling backwards, Mike lost his balance landing harshly on his bottom. As he was standing up to have another go at Frank, Martyn and Andy grabbed an arm each to keep him seated. Mike not putting up much resistance cursed Frank under his breath.

Having long since worked out that he was wasting his time Frank disappointingly shook his head, turned around and slowly walked back in the direction of his home.

Martyn and Andy each let go of Mike's arms. Telling the others to stay there and wait for him Mike stood up and followed Frank, keeping his distance. He had only been following him for a short time when he felt a coldness that he had never experienced before. The hairs on the back of his neck stood up, making him shudder. Something had followed him, he could sense it, whatever it was, was up and close, right behind him. Half expecting one of the others to be following him he looked behind, there was nothing there, still sensing that something was watching him right up near his face.

That evening there was a knock on Frank's front door. He had just finished putting the dishes away after washing up from his supper. Mike had gone to the local police station and reported Frank. He had followed him to check where he lived before going to the police and reporting him for harassment. The police advised Frank that it was best for everyone concerned that he stayed away from the park when Mike and his friends were there. Charges were not pressed against him, he was told to stop bothering them and that he should count himself lucky that he just received a wrap on the knuckles instead.

It was some years later when Lisa had returned to Beechwood Park. Lisa looked back on her life thinking how much she had missed going there. That visit was different though, not only was she a lot older and wiser but now she fully understood who she was and where she was meant to be. Lisa could finally put the jigsaw together, that was her life and move on without any feeling of regret. It had most definitely been a long and tough journey.

Chapter Three

Growing Up

Lisa grew up in a small mid-terraced house, which was situated on a quiet side road, just away from the busy road that went through the local village of Beechwood. The back garden to that house was beautiful; it could have featured in a gardening magazine. Lisa and Susan were rarely allowed to play in that garden and Elizabeth was most definitely never allowed to hang the washing out, it would only have made John's garden look untidy. Elizabeth would have to take all the family's wet laundry along to the laundrette in her reliable tartan patterned shopping trolley and use the driers there. In a funny sort of way she quite enjoyed it, getting her out of the house, if only for a short while. John cared about his garden more than anything else in the world, it was his pride and joy. Not giving as much, if any, attention to their family home.

Elizabeth was on one of her visits to the laundrette whilst Lisa and Susan were left at home in the back garden one sunny day, both sitting cross-legged on the grass playfully enjoying a game of snap, not causing anybody any trouble when John appeared from nowhere. He had quietly walked through the back door as if to scare them intentionally. The girls not noticing him straight away.

Without any obvious reason John began yelling at them. "Get off that lawn now, you stupid little girls. It's taken me years to get it in such perfect condition. Go and play somewhere else." Calming down, an idea had popped into his head, a huge grin appearing on his face before he continued,

"I know, I've had a brilliant idea. Why don't you go and collect registration plates from moving vehicles, preferably on the motorway?"

Lisa jumped right out of her skin; John often had that effect on her. He was no gentle giant, being a tall well-built man with a shaven head, dark brown eyes and having a square jaw, which was, more often than not, covered with stubble.

Lisa and Susan picked up the playing cards before he had chance to shout again. Putting them back in the pack they stood up with their heads still down, neither making eye contact with him. Walking past him they felt his hand around the back of their heads. Lisa walked through the house and straight back out again through the front door, whilst Susan walked up the stairs and straight into their bedroom.

The family who lived next door, had been out in their garden and witnessed John's outburst. Stan, who was the father, was wearing a black and white pin striped apron and had been cooking burgers and sausages for his family, on their barbeque. He was a placid short slim spectacled man and a family man who took pride in everything that he did. John was not his favourite person and had always found it difficult to get along with him. Giving him a quick sideways glance of disapproval, he followed it with a little shake of his head and rolling upwards of the eyeballs. Stan's wife, Maxine, had been trying to relax on her sun lounger, still recovering from the previous day's retail therapy, where she had been shopping for holiday clothes. She was a little taller and more rotund than her husband. Sitting up, revealing a little bit too much for a woman of her age, to see what the commotion was about. Looking over at Stan, she gave out a big sigh before laying back down again and resuming her position. Their two boys, Gareth and Glenn had stopped splashing about in their paddling pool and squirting each other with their water blasters, both looked sad for Lisa and Susan. They were polite young men who had just the right amount of cheekiness. Initially looking and feeling uncomfortable, the family continued to relax and enjoy themselves, once John had gone back indoors that is.

Lisa was now sitting on the garden bench at the front of the house. John allowed them to sit there as long as they kept to the flagged area and did not walk in the flowerbeds or the rockeries. It had been a pleasant warm day that day but when it had been raining the puddles always appeared in the same places on the front garden flags. The stone had worn and weathered over many years. Lisa was in a trance and looking in the direction of where the puddles usually were, a dried green circular pattern of various shades had been left behind. Finding it therapeutic, she listened to the gentle waters of the nearby stream, which flowed out of sight, behind the trees, at the bottom of the garden.

Sitting there for a while longer, she thought about what she could do next. Standing up she looked through the front living room window, all she could see was the back of John's head. He was pre-occupied with one of his favourite pastimes, watching the square box in the corner of the room. Lisa decided to keep out of John's way a little while longer. Walking to the bottom of the garden she ducked underneath the lower branches of a tree before jumping over the stream. Clambering up onto the dry-stone wall alongside the stream she walked on it, slowing down and taking extra care over the loose stones. Walking as far as was possible she turned back around, walking back and jumped back down, the water splashing the front of her legs.

38

Constant reminders about how Susan was the pretty one, were of little help to Lisa's already low self-esteem. Susan was the spitting image of John whilst Lisa looked more like Elizabeth. Not only did they not look anything alike they also had very different personalities. Susan was the fortunate one later in life too. She met, fell in love and married Karl Jones and they started having their family pretty much straight away. They were blessed with two beautiful daughters, Stacey and Jayne, who both looked like Karl. They both attended a private school, although different to the one where their parents taught. Susan a Primary School Teacher and Karl being the Headmaster, at the same school.

Rain clouds were now overhead so Lisa decided not to go to the park. Instead, she could either sit in the living room with John or go up to her bedroom. Choosing the latter, she decided to do a little reading. Opening up the front door she went back into the house, quietly walking past John so as not to disturb his viewing.

Lisa never looked forward to the colder months, wishing her life away, looking forward to the warmer months. She spent most of her time just trying to keep warm, that and trying to avoid the rest of her family. Lisa longed for a bit of privacy but that was impossible when she shared a bedroom with Susan.

The bitter wind would whistle through the gap underneath the bottom of Lisa and Susan's bedroom window frame. It was made of wood and had slowly been rotting away over the years. The gap was big enough that Lisa could poke her fingers all the way through. Any loose pieces of rotten wood would be picked out first before sticking bits of old rags or anything else that would fit, to try to reduce the draught.

One morning Lisa had woken, it was bitterly cold, getting out of bed she got dressed, putting on plenty of layers. Sitting on the wooden window bottom, trying to avoid the splinters, she tried to melt the thick leafed frost pattern on the inside of the window panes. In turn, she used first her fingertip and then her hand on the frosty pattern. The frost would melt leaving behind a see-through patch, when peeking through to the outside she noticed that the frost was everywhere that she looked. Susan had woken and joined Lisa. Opening her mouth wide, Susan breathed onto the window pane, the vapour coming out of her mouth was visible. Lisa and Susan put their index and middle fingers to their lips and pulled them away, pretending to smoke, exhaling the vapour in a sophisticated manner.

The never-ending seasons of heavy rain would always wake Lisa up in the middle of the night. Her first instinct when waking would be to check to make sure that it was not herself that had wet the bed. At certain times of the year, this would be an almost nightly occurrence. Her bedding would still be wet when she climbed back into bed the following evening. Because of the lack of sleep, Lisa would walk around the following day resembling a zombie. Either the teachers did not notice or they simply were not interested when she fell asleep in their lessons.

Lisa had accidentally woken Susan from her sleep. "Are you okay Lisa?"

"It's raining again." Lisa was trying to catch her breath and reposition her bed at the same time. Placing a container underneath each drip, her manoeuvres were

40

done as quietly as were possible. A number of plastic containers were left in their bedroom for such occasions, piled up in one corner of the room. She would empty the containers the following morning or if they became full, whichever occurred first. Under no circumstances were John and Elizabeth to be woken up. The roof had leaked for many years in the same areas above Lisa's bed. The stained ceiling had been evidence of that. Instead of repairing the leaks, they would be covered with yet another layer of paint.

"What time is it?" Susan said, putting her hand over her mouth to stifle a yawn.

"It's just gone three, try and go back to sleep. I've sorted everything." Lisa now feeling wide-awake was unsure if she would be able to get back to sleep.

Susan's bed was in such a position that she did not have to move her bed away from the dripping ceiling. On the downside, she was underneath the draughty window. At particularly breezy times, the curtains could be seen blowing towards her.

Lisa climbed back into her bed, which was now positioned near to the middle of the room. Only a short time had elapsed when Susan started her complaining. "I can't sleep, that dripping noise is really annoying me."

"Shush, just try." The dripping noise had gone beyond annoying Lisa too, taking her to the brink of insanity. Shivering from the cold she also had to contend with the rainwater, which had soaked all the way through her blankets. With no spares and nowhere else for her to go she managed to position herself at the edge of the mattress where it was drier. Feeling weary again, she closed her eyes and drifted back off to sleep.

Lisa and Susan frequently squabbled about petty things. Sharing a portable television which had poor picture quality where the indoor aerial, which was fixed to the television, had snapped off partway down. It was very rare that Lisa managed to win one of their squabbles, being more timid than Susan, who had always been more quick-witted. On those rare occasions when she did and got to watch what she wanted on that television, Susan would put a record on to annoy Lisa more, always to get the last word in. The music would steadily get louder, notch upon notch, until it would drown out the sound of whatever Lisa was watching on the television. Depending on what moods they were both in it would either result in them physically fighting and knocking the living daylights out of each other or Lisa giving in and turning the television off.

Susan had copious amounts of clothing, way more than Lisa, hand-me-downs being the main reason. Only having an old post-war chest of drawers that they shared, to store them in, being allowed two drawers each, Lisa would often have her drawer space stolen and find her clothes ripped up underneath her bed. Susan would mostly do this because she was tired of having hand-me-downs and to vent her frustrations after being told off by John. The atmosphere would more often than not be electric, fully charged with tension.

John worked very long hours in a warehouse and was the main breadwinner. He set off to work before anyone else had even got out of bed each morning, not arriving back home until way after seven in the evenings. Elizabeth was a housewife and also worked part-time hours in a restaurant kitchen, various shifts, but mainly in the evening. John and Elizabeth both worked very hard, but they never appeared to have anything to show for it. There would more often than not be a period of time each day when John and Elizabeth's shifts overlapped, Lisa and Susan would be left in the house by themselves for long periods of time. Without any parental guidance came lots of sibling rivalry.

Susan and Lisa were like chalk and cheese. Susan, the extrovert, was far more confident than Lisa, not caring what people thought or said about her. The adventurous one who enjoyed trying out new hairstyles and the latest colours.

Lisa was introverted, painfully shy and cared very much what people thought about her, she longed for others to like her. She had always wanted a best friend, which most other people seemed to have. Not at all adventurous and never daring, preferring to keep things plain and simple, that way she was less likely to get it wrong and others would not feel it necessary to comment.

One late afternoon Lisa had caught sight of Susan swigging from a whisky bottle. She was laying down at the top of the garden merrily singing songs, like the ones that they sang in morning assembly when they were at junior school. Without a care in the world, Susan had gone straight to a friend's house after school, getting herself into a right state. Reeking of cigarettes as well as the whisky, she was easily lead and would have done anything to keep in with the in-crowd. Susan had decided to go home and carried on drinking by herself, which was what had caused Lisa the most concern.

Lisa had managed to persuade Susan to go into the house and up to their bedroom, where she laid down on her bed. Pouring away the remains of the whisky Lisa threw the empty bottle in next door's dustbin. Susan was sitting on the edge of her bed when Lisa returned.

"I'm going to have to tell Dad when he gets home from work, you know that don't you?" Lisa always found it necessary to take on a maternal role. "It's for your own good. He will probably be able to smell you as soon as he comes through the front door anyway."

Susan slurred but still managed to string a sentence together. "Tell him, I don't give a shit. I'll tell him what you get up to in his greenhouse. What you have done with lots of boys in his greenhouse."

Lisa unsure why she was so surprised at Susan's childish response. "What…what are you talking about now? You're drunk. Stop making up lies. I'm just trying to look out for you."

Susan's 'could not care less' expression let Lisa know exactly what she thought about her. "I'm not drunk, I can handle my alcohol, thank you very much. I'm not lying either… You're the liar. Anyway just shut up, why do you think you can always tell me what to do? You are not my mother."

Lisa tried to get the argument back onto what the issue was really about whilst feeling slightly surprised with how well Susan could talk, be it rather slowly, she was quite obviously used to drinking alcohol. She was even better at twisting an argument to make out that it was the other person that was always in the wrong.

Wanting to help her sister, she ignored the immaturity and continued. "You shouldn't be drinking, but I guess you already know that, don't you? Where did you get the alcohol from and how the hell did you pay for it? Why are you drinking, especially alone? If there is something wrong you can talk to me you know, about absolutely anything."

Susan frowned and was obviously tired of all the questioning. "Listen to you. What's with all the questions? Little miss perfect. You shouldn't be kissing boys in Dad's greenhouse."

"Oh shut up, you stupid girl!" Lisa's patience had now snapped. "I'm just trying to help you but the only thing you seem interested in is self-destruction. Go ahead, drink yourself to death. See if I care."

Susan had always been a bad-tempered character, even when sober, eventually mellowing as she got older. Susan launched herself at Lisa, throwing some really hard punches, her aim particularly accurate considering that she had been drinking. Lisa managed to defend herself quite well up until that last punch, which was particularly brutal. Susan pulled Lisa's hair back, which forced her head to go back. That punch caught Lisa right between her eyes, where she literally saw stars, just like the illustrations in a comic strip. Susan let go of Lisa's hair, which caused Lisa to lose her balance and stumble backwards. Lying flat on her back Lisa managed to catch her breath before Susan went for her again. Lisa was dazed but had to be ready for round two. When Susan tried to kick Lisa she retaliated by getting both legs together, above her and with all her strength she push kicked Susan a good few feet up into the air. In what appeared to be slow motion, Susan finally crash-landed onto the floor right onto her bottom with an almighty thud.

Lisa caught sight of what appeared to be a small orb shaped ball of light, out of the corner of her eye. Turning her head quickly she noted that it had flown through the bedroom door and had vanished into their bedroom table.

On that table, where the television and record player were, was an old jam jar that had a few pens and pencils in. They started to spin around the edge of the rim of the jar, the jam jar remaining perfectly still and not moving once.

Susan turned and looked straight at the jar. Both were still shaking from the adrenaline rush. Susan stood bolt upright whilst Lisa slowly walked backwards and lowered herself so that she was sitting on the edge of her bed. The pens and pencils continued to spin at the same speed, the jar never moving. Susan slowly approached the jar to have a closer look, where she felt that she was pushed from behind. It was not a hard push but it was enough that she lost her balance slightly. With that, Susan fell forward against the broken television aerial and cut her neck at the side. "Ouch." Susan put her fingers up to her neck, checking for blood. Even though it smarted, it was only a surface scratch. Susan turned around and was about to continue the fight with Lisa, she noticed that Lisa was still sat on her bed. Lisa looked straight back at Susan with bewilderment in her eyes, she had not actually moved.

Without saying another word, Susan got out a cardboard box, which she had decorated with flowery wrapping paper, from behind her bed and started to look through her record collection. Picking up her magazine Lisa laid on her bed flicking through the pages, not really absorbing the content. It was only after a short while, once they had stopped arguing and the atmosphere in the bedroom had returned to normal that the pens and pencils stopped spinning. All was back to near normal, like nothing had happened. Lisa found an old can of air-freshener under the kitchen sink and sprayed the house with it whilst Susan rubbed some toothpaste on her teeth and ate a teaspoonful to try to disguise the smell of alcohol. Surprisingly Susan was not sick but she did go straight to sleep without eating her evening meal. Lisa and Susan never mentioned anything to their parents about the alcohol, argument or what had happened afterwards either. When Lisa was asked about her black eye, she explained that it was a fight that she had got into at school.

It was only a few days later when they had been having yet another one of their petty disagreements. John's black leather belt, which was hanging up by its buckle on the hook on the back of their bedroom door, suddenly and without any warning started to swing against the back of the door. They had only just started to squabble, it was about something and nothing, not much tension had been created and no punches had been exchanged. The belt had been put there to remind them that if they misbehaved then John could easily retrieve it and they would feel it quickly wrapped around their bottoms.

It was not a gradual movement, it went from being perfectly still to swaying like there was no tomorrow. The belt had not been touched and nobody had been anywhere near the door to make it happen. It hit the door frame on each side whilst the buckle remained on the hook, keeping up a regular tempo. Without warning, it stopped dead.

Elizabeth was a thin pale lady who looked like she was scared of her own shadow. Her brown greasy hair always looked like it needed a good cut. She wore glasses that did not sit properly on her nose and were much too big for her face. Elizabeth would often threaten Lisa and Susan by saying, "Just wait until your father gets home. He'll sort you both out." They would spend the next few hours praying that Elizabeth would not say anything to John, not wanting yet another good hiding. Preferring to keep things calm most of the time she rarely told him, the fear itself was punishment enough.

Unexplained incidents only occurred when the adults were not present. Ornaments would often fly horizontally from the mantel piece, travelling with some speed horizontally through the air up to a certain distance and drop vertically straight to the ground. Strangely, there were never any breakages.

Occasionally witnessing ghostly figures, a young girl dressed in period clothing wandered about the house, most often noticed walking down the staircase. An old man had been seen sitting in John's chair, which was the nearest to the fire. He would be leaning forward and picking at what appeared to be scabs on his legs. He did not wander about in the house; he was only ever seen sitting in that chair. Whistling of old wartime tunes could be heard coming from the direction of the chair. They never discussed it with anyone else, presuming it was normal and other people saw the same things.

Their bedroom had been in a poor state of repair. Badly decorated was an understatement, the wallpaper and paint were peeling off. Lisa would pick at the loose bits with her badly bitten fingernails when she was bored, nobody able to tell the difference. She would try to hide the bad decoration with posters of any pop stars from her magazines.

Always feeling hungry when getting home from school, she would check the kitchen cupboards and fridge, already knowing that they would be empty. Elizabeth would go to the local corner shop daily to only buy what was needed for that particular day's evening meal. It was not always a filling meal but Elizabeth did the best that she could with the small amount of money that she had earned. It was always good wholesome food but the portions would be small.

The wall between Lisa and Susan's bedroom and that of John and Elizabeth's was a paper-thin partition wall. Almost every night Lisa would hear her parents having sex. Elizabeth's moaning and John's grunting would also greet her as she awoke in the mornings too. Pressing one ear down onto her mattress she would put the pillow over her other ear. The mattress was old, thin and very uncomfortable, the springs regularly poking her in the ribs. Pressing her arm down over the pillow, she would try to block out the noises that made her feel disgusted. Not always doing the trick, this did not drown out the noises as their headboard would bang against the wall, echoing like a kettledrum along with the sound of their bellies slapping together.

Even though there was quite an age gap between Lisa and Susan they were always made to go up to bed at the same time. Bedtimes were always early, every night, making no difference if it was a school night or not. Most nights Lisa never even felt tired and would lay there for hours hiding from the lurking shadows.

No matter what time of the year Lisa's bed always had lots of covers on, making it feel like there was a heavy weight on top of her. In the warmer months, she would take some of the covers off, fold them and tuck them under her bed. Elizabeth would put them back on the bed the following day.

Suffering with arachnophobia, Lisa found it nearly impossible to use their outside toilet, everyone else she knew had a toilet in their bathroom. Even more spiders would take up residence in the outhouse in the colder months. Not only did she have to contend with the spiders but the toilet seat would be freezing. It was always the same routine, first checking for the eight legged creatures, pulling down her knickers, bracing herself, holding her breath, then on three sitting straight down on the freezing toilet seat and gasping for breath. The toilet door had never closed properly either. Lisa would have to put one leg out in front of her to ensure that she was not seen whilst ensuring that any bodily fluids were directed into the water and not down her leg. Soft toilet paper was non-existent in their household; instead, there would be a soggy newspaper where she would have to tear off a piece when she needed to wipe herself. If nobody else was about she would urinate around the back of the outhouse instead. Some nights whilst lying in bed, she would need the toilet, preferring to wait until morning before going.

Lisa did not like getting up when it was dark, sensing that something was staring through the bedroom door at her, never daring to look back. Lisa would lay there, pretending to be asleep, whilst everyone else was tucked up in bed sleeping soundly.

The living room was the nicest room in the house. It was not perfect but it was the only room that looked like someone had made an attempt to decorate it. The furniture was not too bad in there either. It felt comfortable and was the only warm room in the winter because it had a fire. The only downside was that Lisa had to sit with her family in that room if she wanted to keep warm.

After having a really busy day Elizabeth had to finish her day preparing an evening meal for the family before going out to work an evening shift. One evening John slammed through the front door after an obvious bad day at work, flopping into the chair without first taking off his shoes, getting changed or having a wash. No sooner had he sat down than Elizabeth appeared from the kitchen with his meal on a tray, putting it down on his lap for him.

"How was your day at work, John?" Elizabeth smiled at him and ignored the fact that he had forgotten his manners. She leant forward to give him a kiss.

John moved away from her, choosing to snap at her instead. "What a stupid question. How do you think my day was?"

Not wishing to continue with that conversation any more Elizabeth moved away from him and got ready to go to work, looking nervous as she tied the laces on her shoes. Lisa and Susan had already finished eating and were upstairs in their bedroom, laying on their beds, doing their homework.

John stood up with the plate in his right hand, the tray dropping to the floor. "Are you trying to kill me, you stupid woman? This food is not cooked properly." Elizabeth instinctively knew that she needed to duck down as the plate flew over her head. There was absolutely nothing wrong with the food, he just wanted somebody to vent his frustrations out on. The liver, onions, mash, peas, gravy and broken plate were now either randomly stuck to the wall or on the carpet.

Elizabeth gave out a little sigh, she was already going to be late for work but she would need to clean up his mess first.

She felt John's fist hit her in the eye. He leant over her and shook his clenched hand in her face. "Don't sigh at me again or you'll get another one to match that one."

Elizabeth already clearly shaken, got up from the floor and went into the kitchen to get the bin and a damp cloth. It would need to be cleaned up properly later, when she got back from work. After years of experience, she knew better than to make any further comments and gave no indication as to what she was thinking with her blank facial expression.

Before putting on her coat she dashed upstairs and covered up her bruising with concealer and put on a pair of sunglasses.

Lisa and Susan had heard the commotion. They knew it was for the best that they stayed in their room and did not make a sound.

John, appearing much calmer, sat back down and put the television on. Elizabeth walked past John on her way out through the front door. Closing the front door gently she left for work.

Every Saturday afternoon John would make his family sit down together to watch the television. It would either have been sport, news or a wild life documentary. If any of the family had got too noisy John would shout for them to shut up whilst turning up the television even louder, to drown out their noise. They were made to sit still, John would sound like a stuck record when repeatedly saying, "Children should be seen and not heard."

Whilst watching television a hint of a cleavage or a full breast frontal left Lisa cringing with embarrassment. Knowing what would follow made Lisa feel so sad for

Elizabeth too, nobody ever having the nerve to stand up to John.

"Wow look at the tits on that. I wish your mother had a pair like that," John would say. His remark did not appear to be aimed at anybody in particular. Elizabeth would not look at John, she would just look at her girls whilst smiling and shrug her shoulders, hiding the torture and putting on a brave face for the sake of Lisa and Susan, only crying later when she was alone.

Their family holidays were never anything to write home about, staying in the same grotty flat every time they went to Cleethorpes. Never going away in the summertime, they were possibly the palest children in their school. John would get up early each morning to go to the local newsagents for his morning paper and forty cigarettes for that day, waking everybody else with his banging around. Some days smoking them all before the evening meal so he would have to go out again in the evening to buy more. Elizabeth would stay behind in the flat to look after Lisa and Susan. In the mornings once they had risen out of their beds and got themselves ready they would sit still whilst Elizabeth prepared a full English breakfast for them all. John would always take his time at the newsagents. When he returned he would sit down in the armchair and open up his newspaper. Elizabeth would never ask him why it had taken him so long, it was only a two minute walk to the nearest newsagent. He would glance at the headlines and pay particular attention to the naked girl on page three. When he had finished with his paper, he would fold it up and place it on top of the coffee table. Like clockwork, he picked up the remote control and put the news on the television, never speaking until he had completed his morning routine. Once breakfast had been eaten, Elizabeth cleared away after everybody. Most of the morning would be spent sitting around either waiting for the rain to stop or waiting to see if John had actually got anything planned for that day. If they did go out, the whole family would get back in time so that John could have a lunchtime nap. Elizabeth, Lisa and Susan would tiptoe around the flat whilst he slept so as not to waken him. John would not allow Elizabeth to venture out by herself, especially not with Lisa and Susan. After John's nap and lunch the whole family would either go for a walk along the seafront or in the park.

Lisa was envious of some of the other children in her class at school; they used to always go abroad, some of them more than once a year. They would go on aeroplanes and always came back with beautiful glowing tans. One girl in their class, Yvonne always seemed to have an all year round tan. Lisa had never even seen an aeroplane up close, let alone been inside one. Some of the other children never strayed out of the country either.

Lisa found life disappointing and felt like she had missed out on a lot, never being invited to parties but witnessing the invitations being given out and hearing the excitement, before and after each event. When wishing them a happy birthday, they would just pleasantly smile and say "thank you."

Christmas was a time of year that Lisa loved the most, always an exciting time when the family would get together. She only saw some of her family at Christmas because they lived quite a distance away.

Elizabeth's parents had lived in Spain for many years. Grandad Buckley wanted to live somewhere warm. He had arthritis and the warmer weather made it much more bearable. Grandma Buckley just wanted to live wherever her husband wanted to be and would have followed him up to the moon, Christmas always being spent in their hometown though. They were always generous, affectionate grandparents who gave out lots of kisses and cuddles, which Lisa and Susan always made the most of.

John originated from Cornwall, where his parents remained. John met Elizabeth when she was on holiday down there with her parents. They always tried to convince everyone that it was love at first sight, knowing that they had to get married because of Elizabeth's impending arrival of Lisa.

Grandma and Grandad Parkins were not quite as generous and were much stricter, nearly, but not quite regimental. It is not that they did not have any money, they just did not like to part with it. Christmas always seemed like such a chore to them, appearing obliged to go for their dinner, not waiting for it all to be over.

Grandad Parkins was a miserable old bugger and had been noted saying "waste of bloody money, commercialised load of rubbish. Most of these young ones today don't even know what Christmas is really about."

One year he had Lisa and Susan in floods of tears when he told them that Santa was fed up with the government and the state of the country, so he had committed suicide. John found it hilarious and was in hysterics. Elizabeth on the other hand did not find it funny and it took her quite a while to convince the girls that their grandad had only been joking.

Grandad Parkins never complained about Elizabeth's cooking though and managed to demolish that year on year.

Once everybody had arrived in the morning, they would all sit round in a circle exchanging gifts. Lisa and Susan always received a lot more presents than anyone else. They would be squeezing and rattling their presents as they tried to work out what was inside. Grandad Buckley always helped with putting the new toys or gadgets together whilst Grandma Buckley would be tidying away all the gift wrap, tags and ribbons. Grandma and Grandad Parkins would sit there and never make any attempts to help with anything, instead they would sit and wait for their lunches to be served.

All the grown-ups would start drinking early whilst chatting away and catching up on everything that had been going on. John even appeared to be happy. Elizabeth would be hurrying around the kitchen, getting a little too merry on the free flowing wine whilst preparing the dinner. There would be the sound of laughter and the feel of a happy atmosphere. The radio would be playing Christmas tunes in the morning whilst everybody opened their gifts.

The fire would be blazing whilst they sat round eating their Christmas dinner. It was magical when it snowed, even if just a little flurry. The only day of the year when Lisa did not want the sun to shine. The lunch was always an impressive feast; it was the same every year. There would be the usual dates and twiglets to nibble on, that was before they had even started their dinner. They never had a starter, they did not really need one. If they had, they would not have had enough room for dessert. John always brought a massive turkey through from the kitchen, it was his job to carve it. Lisa often thought how funny it would be if he tripped over when he was carrying it through. The leftovers from the turkey would last for a few days after. They always had sage and onion stuffing, Yorkshire puddings, seasonal vegetables and gravy with the turkey.

It did not matter how much Lisa managed to eat, when she looked down at her plate the food portion never seemed to get any smaller. Dessert was Christmas pudding; the adults had brandy sauce with it and the children could choose between custard and ice cream. When everyone had finished Elizabeth would fetch out the coffee with cheese and biscuits. Lisa would chuckle when Grandad Parkins fell asleep straight after his lunch.

"You could set your watch by him." John was convinced that it was too coincidental, that he was pretending to be asleep so that it got him out of helping with the washing up. After lunch, once all the clearing and washing-up had been done everybody would watch the Queens speech and settle down to watch a movie.

Christmas Day would always be over too quickly. Lisa would always feel a little twinge of sadness when the family had to leave.

On birthdays, Elizabeth would make Lisa a cake and hand make a birthday card for her. John and Elizabeth would put a small amount of money inside the card. Lisa would buy something for herself with the money, which would be nearly always magazines and chocolates. Lisa kept every one of those birthday cards, which she tucked away in a shoebox at the bottom of her wardrobe.

Lisa and Susan would get a chocolate Easter egg each from their closest relatives. Never being allowed to eat chocolate during lent they would always keep them until

Easter Sunday. The eggs were kept on top of a welsh dresser and it was torture for Lisa looking at all that chocolate every day. When the day arrived, she would eat chocolate until she felt sick. Easter Sunday, Christmas day and birthdays were the only days that they were allowed to over indulge in anything sweet like chocolate.

Punishment came all too often and more often than not seemed far too severe. There was no room for second chances in their house, which is why Lisa spent most of her childhood scared of John.

One such punishment had come one Sunday morning when Lisa had woken up earlier than usual and put the television on. She had been watching and following a series called 'Around the World in Eighty Days by Phileas Fogg and Passepartout'. Putting on the right channel, she would lay in her bed and wait for it to come on. The volume was on really low so as not to disturb anybody, John somehow still managed to hear it.

"Lisa, get in this bloody room now." His voice bellowed around the house. He did not seem to care that he would wake Elizabeth and Susan up.

Susan awoke and her snoring stopped, with her puffy eyes she looked over at Lisa with bewilderment on her face. Lisa got up out of her bed and went over to the television to switch if off before slowly walking into her parents' bedroom with her head held low.

"Get in that corner, face the wall and put your hands on your head." John's voice a little too loud for early morning commands. "Do not speak or move until I tell you that you can. Am I making myself clear?"

"Yes, Dad," Lisa answered without any trace of attitude, not wanting to aggravate the situation.

She was tired of being punished and found it even more upsetting that she had missed that particular episode, never getting to see it again either, it was never to be repeated. Lisa had been stood there for some time, her arms and legs had become numb, trying to move, only very slightly, so as not to be noticed. The sensation of pins and needles had started to set in, moving without permission would result in further more severe punishment. Susan had been known to join Lisa on a few occasions for crimes they were supposed to have committed, be it separately or together.

John laid there, in his bed, his head resting on a pillow whilst chain smoking. Elizabeth would be laid there at his side, like his obedient servant, who did not dare to speak out against him. There was very little ventilation in that bedroom and it was full to the ceiling with cigarette fumes. A tiny gap under the window was not enough for that amount of smoke to escape. Lisa found it hard to control herself, trying her hardest not to cough, feeling the urge to blink more, her eyes being sore and red. The ashtray at the side of John was already overflowing with cigarette ends, with ash all over the duvet, at the side of the bed and on the floor. Lisa tried her best not to overbalance and touch the bedroom walls that had a nicotine coating on.

John sat up, resting his cigarette in the ashtray he reached underneath him and threw his pillow across the room aiming it at Lisa, landing and hitting her at the back of her head causing her to lose her balance and crack her face against the wall. "Right, you've had plenty of time to think about what you've done wrong. In future, young lady, if you wake up early on a Sunday morning you lay in bed until I tell you that you can get up. You do not turn the television on and disturb the rest of the house. Am I making myself clear?"

"Yes, Dad." Somehow managing not to cry, her eyes had begun to fill with tears.

"Go on, get out of my sight." His loud voice booming around the room.

Making sure that he did not see her tears Lisa moved out of the room quicker than what she had gone in, going back to her own bed. Susan was still lying in her bed, the covers were tucked up and underneath her chin. Looking at Lisa with pity in her tired eyes Susan had noticed a large bump appearing above Lisa's left eyebrow. Lisa smiled at Susan whilst rubbing her arms and legs trying to get the pins and needles sensation to go away quicker. Getting back into bed, Lisa laid there remaining perfectly still. Susan turned over and tried to go back to sleep.

"Arghh. Bloody hell." John jumped up out of bed. He had picked his cigarette back up out of the ashtray, somehow it had turned around in the ashtray and he had put the lit end against his lip, a blister appearing straight away. Neither Susan nor Lisa dared to move. Elizabeth jumped up straight away, went downstairs to the fridge to get some butter to put on his lip.

Lisa was fifteen years old when she had to avoid showers after a games lesson yet again. "Grab a towel and get yourself into the shower Lisa." Miss Aitken, a short stocky teacher with a crew cut, would always stand at the end of the showers as though getting into that shower was a life or death situation.

"Sorry, miss, I can't today. I'm on my period." Lisa not making eye contact with her teacher, instead she looked over at the towels, which were the size of handtowels and would only cover up your modesty.

Her chubby finger, which revealed a badly bitten fingernail, moved down her register to check. "You were on your period last week, Lisa."

"My periods are very irregular, miss, they are all over the place. I'm sorry, miss, I can't help it." Lisa, along with most of the other girls, used this excuse knowing that Miss Aitken nor any of the other teachers would ever ask any of the girls to prove it.

"Okay, Lisa, I'll mark it down on the register." Miss Aitken tilted her head slightly and gave her a knowing look.

In reality Lisa was a late developer and had not even started her periods, she was just simply trying to hide the fact that she was covered in bruises. Her bottom and lower back were black and blue, it had started to fade a little bit. Getting changed in one of the toilet cubicles so that the other girls did not see, Lisa thought that it was easier to cover up the truth than have to explain things to others whilst they pointed their fingers at her.

Two weeks previously, a minor incident had occurred at home and neither Lisa nor Susan could admit to it. An empty milk bottle had somehow been broken on the front door step. The fact that it could have been done by an animal or fallen over by itself never seemed to cross John's mind. There would never have been a chance to discuss this either.

"Lisa, come here now. Pull your knickers down and bend over my knee." John appeared to have a glint in his eye, as though it gave him some type of perverse pleasure.

Lisa walked slowly towards him trying to reason with him. "Please, no, Dad. It wasn't me, I swear."

Reaching out and grabbing her tightly by her wrist, he pulled up her skirt and tore her knickers when he pulled them down with force. Taking his slipper off, he bent Lisa over his knee and forcefully smacked her several times, the bruising was almost instant. Pushing her off his knee Lisa fell to the floor, landing straight on both of her kneecaps. Standing up with her knickers still around her knees, the tears were in full flow rolling down her face as her knickers fell to her ankles.

John had decided that it was his fatherly duty to take it upon himself to hit Lisa and Susan with a slipper in turn until one of them owned up to it. Whilst John was laying into Susan she looked up and over at Lisa, as though trying to convey that she needed her help with much sadness in her eyes. Lisa knew from that look that Susan was as innocent as she was.

The pain had become too raw and excruciating for Lisa after several turns and it was obvious that Susan was not going to own up to it either. She could no longer take any more physical or mental abuse.

"I did it." Lisa said without giving herself any more time to think about it. "I'm sorry, Dad, it was an accident. I didn't mean to do it."

"At last. You finally have the courage to admit to it." John continued to hit her with the palm of his hand, a slap with every word. "Do-not-ever-tell-me-any-lies-again-or-you-will-get-it-twice-as-hard-next-time." A short pause where Lisa thought and hoped that John had finished. "Do-you-understand?"

"Yes, Dad." Lying over John's knee her skin was stinging unbearably, her flesh feeling like it was on fire. A panicked feeling came over Lisa as she noticed that she suddenly needed to go to the toilet desperately and could no longer hold her bladder. Not daring to ask if she could go, it was all over in a flash as she noticed that she was wet and worse still, so was John. Lisa cried uncontrollably. Again John pushed Lisa off his knee, managing to put her hands out this time as she fell to the floor, managing to save her knees.

"You dirty little bitch; you've pissed all over me. Why the hell are you crying, just shut up or I'll really give you something to cry about. Get out of my sight now before I do something that I will really regret." John was thoroughly disgusted with her as he screwed up his face whilst looking down his nose at his trousers.

Lisa felt so sad that she wished she could just die, there and then. Immediately pulling up what was left of her knickers, she left the room before John could say anything else to her. He did not follow her, Susan did. She followed Lisa to their bedroom. Lisa was still crying when Susan went up to her and put her arms around her. Hugging each other tight, they cried without saying anything.

Lisa had always tried so hard to make John proud of her, nothing was ever good enough for him though. Finally realising that she was onto a losing battle when she overheard John talking to Elizabeth one night when she was going downstairs to get a glass of water.

"Please don't be like that John," Elizabeth pleaded with him.

"If she hadn't come along I could have been a doctor by now. That girl ruined any chance of me having a career. We could be living a much better life than this one." John spoke down to her, sounding more like he was trying to convince himself than Elizabeth.

"I know it was an unplanned pregnancy but we can't turn back the clocks. We have to make the most of what we have. I'm happy, why can't you be?" Sounding like she could burst into tears at any given moment.

"We should have listened to my parents; you should have had an abortion. They practically begged us." His voice full of regret and loathing.

Lisa could not listen any more, she tiptoed back up to her room. Getting back into bed, she curled up on her side and wept quietly, so as not to waken Susan.

Susan had never allowed Lisa to hang around with her or any of her friends. Neither did she stick up for her when she was being bullied, especially on the school bus. It got so bad at one point that Lisa started to avoid looking at her own reflection at all, be it a mirror, a shop window or anything else. She started to walk to and from school by herself to avoid the school bus even if the weather was bad, crossing over the road when necessary to avoid the gangs.

On one occasion it was particularly daunting, it was the last time that Lisa ever caught the school bus and clearly remembers the taunting from the other pupils who were sitting behind her, not even knowing who some of them were.

"Freaky Lisa." The name-calling and chanting had started. Coming close up right behind her, she could feel their breath moving her hair.

Another said, "Lisa smells all yeasty."

Whilst others said, "Oxfam reject Lisa." The ones that weren't name calling were laughing.

Acting like a pack of wolves, the name-calling continued. Never letting it show how deeply she was hurting, she carried on looking straight ahead and pretended that it was not happening. Her bus stop was fast approaching, part of her wanted to run off the bus but upon standing up, she realised that she was too tense for that, her knees did not seem to want to bend either. The verbal abuse continued from out of the back bus windows long after she had got off. One of the bullies threw something at her out of the window, it was a pencil sharpener that they got right on target, bouncing off the back of Lisa's head. Not hurting her physically too much, emotionally a wreck inside with nobody that she could turn to, she went straight to the park until she could face going home. The two main culprits were not exactly gifted in the looks department either, the boy was lanky and had goofy teeth and the girl had bright ginger wiry hair, which appeared to have a mind of its own. However, they fitted in with the in-crowd because their parents had money and could afford to buy them nice clothes.

It was only a few days later when Karma intervened. They had decided to do a suicide pact and were both sat in the goofy kid's dad's car in his garage. Waiting for his parents to go out they put a pipe from the exhaust into a slightly opened side window and filled the car with carbon monoxide. They died holding hands.

Worrall Valley High School had been an absolute nightmare and would haunt Lisa for the rest of her life. Being a loner, she would walk around by herself, preferring to hide away from all the losers.

Lisa never looked forward to the games lessons, thinking it unfair when the teachers looked for volunteers to pick their own team members. Initially Lisa had put up her hand to volunteer. Somehow, the popular confident girls would always make it to the front, putting their hands straight up as high as they could.

"Volunteers needed to pick four teams for a rounders' competition," Miss Aitken said.

"Me, miss," Linda, a pretty tall girl with long black silky hair, said in a creepy manner.

"Oh please pick me miss," Alison, who was yet another pretty tall girl, said.

They were chosen along with two other girls. Miss Aitken not appearing to notice that Lisa had also put her hand up. She was unsure if she should feel angry for being ignored yet again or if she should heave with all the creeping around Miss Aitken that was going on. The four girls would then stand at the front and face them, looking all prim and proper and acting like they were on a Miss World beauty competition stage. They would proceed to pick their best friends, the girls who were exceptionally good at games and the leftovers, in that order. Lisa was always the latter, looking like a spare part right up until the end.

Lisa made the reserve bench on the netball team and enjoyed playing hockey, even after a particularly vicious game when she got bruised shins and her ankles swelled up. She tried her hardest when playing rounders and always managed to finish in the top twenty when it came to the cross-country running.

One Parents' Evening at High School was the final straw for Lisa, giving up any hope that John could actually be proud of her. A glowing report from her teachers, the only concern being that she did not join in with class discussions. A very bright student who needed to build up her confidence, low self-esteem issues was the comment from the majority.

The walk home from school after the Parents' Evening with John appeared very quiet and tense, more so than usual. Lisa looked up at John and smiled. No smile was given in return.

"What is it with you, Lisa?" John seemingly genuinely confused.

Lisa looked at John with a blank expression on her face, not understanding what he was asking.

"You just can't do anything right, can you?" His disappointment was evident.

Lisa gave no response, not understanding what it was that she had done that was so wrong on that particular occasion.

Grabbing Lisa's shoulder to stop her from walking he leant right down and over her and ran his sharp facial stubble roughly down the side of her face, making her wince. A tear gently slid down her cheek and over her delicate skin, which had started to look quite sore. Lisa was still confused as they continued to walk home, saying nothing more. No praise was received from Elizabeth either.

Lisa had worked hard at school every day, trying her best at everything. Being ambitious she wanted the big house, nice car and exotic holidays; she wanted to have everything that she never had as a child. Going to university to study to become a doctor was all she had ever dreamt about. By the time she was sixteen she gave up on her long-term dreams. After sitting her exams at school, she decided to leave school and start work instead. Lisa would take any job, as long as it was a paid job. It was time for her to leave home and venture out on her own; she was more than ready for the world outside.

Chapter Four

The Recipe Book

Lisa moved in with one of her work colleagues who had also been looking to move out from her parents' house and fly the nest for some time. Michelle Shaw got on with her parents she just wanted her own place but could not afford to go it alone. They had not known each other for long but they got on pretty well and anything was better than living at home. The landlord allowed them to decorate the house as they wanted it, saving them having to pay a deposit and bond. It was a small house with enough outside space for a dustbin and a length of washing line around the back. Lisa found it exciting that it had a proper bathroom with a toilet and having her own bedroom and space, which was small but at least she could shut out the world whenever she needed to. Michelle had the larger bedroom, flipping a coin to decide who got which bedroom before they had actually moved in.

They shared the bills fifty/fifty, bought their own food, sometimes sharing. To make sure that the housework was shared equally they drew up a rota.

Lisa started to get on really well with Michelle, the more she got to know her, the more she liked her. Michelle appeared to be a lot older than just the couple of years that was between them. Everybody noticed her when she walked into a room with both her good looks and bubbly personality, filling a room with her presence.

Michelle had made the decision that they should have a housewarming party the first Saturday night that they had moved in. Everyone either took a bottle of wine or a pack of lagers. The majority of the people that were there were Michelle's friends, she had lots of crazy friends who knew how to party. It was all new to Lisa and she loved it, feeling relaxed it was not long before she started to feel a little bit tipsy. Drinking alcohol was a whole new experience, only ever having had a couple of sips of lager before. With very little persuasion and making up for lost time Lisa smoked her first joint that night, making her feel a little strange with super hearing, closely followed by the onset of a headache and nausea.

A police van kept driving up and down the road that night. It was not coincidental; one of the neighbours had rung the police to complain. The partygoers were one-step ahead, they had lookouts who would signal them when the police were in sight. The loud rock music would get turned down and the lights would be switched off. It made Lisa chuckle and think about that game that you played at children's parties, 'musical statues'. Even the partygoers outside knew to hide when they saw the lights go off and the music stopped. There was a certain buzz about avoiding a telling off from the police. The party came to a close in the early hours of Sunday morning. Everyone who was at the party crashed at the house, there was no floor space left that did not have a body lying there. Bodies were trying to sleep on the staircase and a couple were squeezed into the bathtub. All night there was a lot of clambering over each other to use the toilet, find more alcohol and drugs or to find somewhere to vomit, nobody getting much sleep.

The house looked like a tornado had swept through it by the time daylight hours arrived; it was well and truly trashed. It was a good job that the redecorating had not been done yet. The guests left slowly in small numbers during the course of the morning until it was just Michelle and Lisa that were left. Nobody volunteered to help with the mess, each guest looking like death warmed up and wanting to go home to their own beds. It was like they had been practicing voodoo or like a scene from a zombie film.

Lisa's head was pounding. She had not had much sleep, a couple of painkillers and some coca cola soon helped her on her way. The amount of empty bottles and cans was staggering, soon losing count after filling the first couple of bin liners. Lisa did not mind clearing up but wretched a few times when it came to clearing up the vomit and the used condoms that were trying to take root on the carpet. All of the windows were opened wide. The smells in the house were disgusting, being a mixture of cannabis, alcohol and vomit mixed in with fart fumes. Lisa and Michelle wrapped tea-towels around the bottom parts of their faces, covering their noses and mouths to try to mask the odours. Taking them most of the afternoon to clean up, by the time they had finished the house smelt more like a hospital. There was nowhere in the house that they could escape to without smelling the bleach fumes, it was more pleasant than the alternatives but overpowering.

Over the following weeks Lisa really started to relax and come out of her shell. She had made some friends and enjoyed her packing job in the factory. It was not the job that she had always dreamt of but she was earning her own money and she had her freedom, nobody was judging her or breathing down her neck anymore. The company that

Lisa worked for was called S.T.A. Sports (Beechwood) Ltd. They packed anything and everything to do with the sporting world. Lisa had started to look forward to the future and the loneliness of her childhood was now slowly becoming a distant memory.

Michelle would sneak Lisa into the nightclubs on Friday and Saturday nights, diverting the bouncers' attention by giving them the come-on with her big green eyes and her very noticeable cleavage, flirting outrageously with them. It never failed and went on week after week. Getting back home at three in the morning was the norm. Never seeing Sunday mornings, finally rising from their beds on a Sunday afternoon, leaving on their pyjamas and recovering before going back to work on the Monday morning. Both were single and enjoying life to the full. Lisa was making up for her sheltered upbringing, working hard and playing hard. The adrenaline, that buzz for life, keeping her going.

One night Lisa was woken from her sleep when she heard voices coming from the bathroom. Turning over she looked at her alarm clock, it read just a little after midnight. Laying still, she questioned herself, she could have been mistaken, the voices could have been coming from outside. The two deep voices started again in a slow deep controlling manner. Michelle was still fast asleep and snoring rhythmically in her bedroom, they had not disturbed her. Lisa continued to lay still, half asleep, trying to work out what they were saying; only catching some of the conversation.

"The girl who lays awake, that is Lisa. She is not to be touched and is to be left alone at all costs." He spoke as though he was the one that gave out the orders.

"Yes I understand. What about her friend though, that is sleeping?" His friend seemingly very interested in Michelle.

"Michelle is Lisa's friend. She is to be left alone too."

The hairs on the back of Lisa's neck stood up. She sat upright thinking that it must be someone that she knew or should know. She did not recognise their voices. How did they get in and what were they going to do, they did not have many possessions to their names for them to be robbed. Lisa was too scared to tackle them by herself anyway.

The voices had stopped. Lisa waited a few moments longer. Getting out of bed, she put on her pink fluffy slippers and dressing gown and tiptoed over to her bedroom door. The door creaked as she opened it, slowly popping her head out through the door opening she was no longer able to hear anything. Michelle was still sound asleep in her room. There was a streetlight directly outside the front of the house, which lit up the upstairs, making it easier to see. The bathroom door had been left open. Tiptoeing across the landing towards the bathroom she needed to confirm to herself that there was nobody in there. It was empty. Keeping her ears open, she crept down the stairs. The living room and kitchen were both empty, there was nowhere for them to possibly hide and all the windows and doors were still locked.

Panic suddenly came over Lisa when she realised that they must have gone into Michelle's room, the only room in the house that she had not checked. Quickly tiptoeing back up the stairs, her heart pounded against her ribcage. Stopping at the top to catch her breath she put her hand over her mouth and managed to stop herself from breathing loudly. There was silence from Michelle's room as Lisa slowly opened her bedroom door. Relief came over her when she realised that the men were not in there either. Michelle was curled up on her side, undisturbed, still fast asleep. Closing Michelle's bedroom door gently behind her Lisa went back to her own room and climbed back into bed.

Not managing to get back to sleep that night she heard Michelle getting up the following morning. She was humming one of those made up tunes whilst she was in the shower. Sounding in good spirits she was obviously feeling refreshed after what Lisa can only presume must have been a good night's sleep. Lisa chose not to mention the voices she had heard in the night.

Later that same day, they decided to start to take it in turns to have the run of the house so that they could invite guests over and make them dinner. The other one would either have to stay in their room or make themselves scarce and go out. Lisa thought that it was really good fun and invited Susan and her family over when it was her turn. She did invite John and Elizabeth on several different occasions, they always made up excuses, so in the end she gave up trying.

Lisa had bought a recipe book *Common-sense Cookery for Wally's* a couple of weeks earlier from a book store in the indoor market. She just loved experimenting and spicing up the recipes. It was Lisa's bible of the cookery world. Michelle would borrow the book from her and do the same with her guests.

Everything was going smoothly, they were working, going out clubbing and having friends and family over to eat when without warning, out of the blue one night,

Michelle seemed really uptight. Lisa had not said or done anything to upset Michelle that she was aware of; her day at work had been good too. Checking the rota Lisa saw that it was her turn to do the vacuuming, she started to pick empty pop bottles from the floor and have a general tidy up first.

"Every time I turn around you're there, getting in my way. Get out of my face. Why don't you go out with your friends or go see your family? Just let me be." Michelle looked angry and her eyes looked different for some reason.

"I'm sorry Michelle." Lisa was confused and could not think of anything else to say, after all, Michelle was the one that always invited Lisa along, wherever she went.

Michelle reached and picked up a small glass vase that had been sat in the centre of the mantelpiece. Aiming it she threw it straight in Lisa's direction whilst screaming. "Arghh you freak."

Lisa's reactions were quick, she ducked down and surprisingly it never hit her. It could not be heard smashing either. Slowly and nervously looking up, Lisa will never forget the look on Michelle's face as she stood there with her mouth gaping open, her facial expression was just one of disbelief.

"What the…it just vanished." Michelle was now acting calmly, like the previous few minutes had never even happened.

Not replying, Lisa was still quite shaken from Michelle's outburst. Lisa thought that the best thing to do was to just leave the room calmly and go up to her room. As she was leaving the room, she heard Michelle repeating herself.

"The vase… it just vanished… into thin air." Her facial expression still one of disbelief.

Things did start to get back to normal after a few days. However, Lisa was still wary of Michelle, keeping out of her way initially. Repeatedly apologising Michelle said that she did not know what had come over her. Lisa never spoke about why Michelle thought she had lost her temper or about the vase episode, which, incidentally, was never seen again after that day.

Not spending break times or lunchtimes at work together any more felt strange to Lisa to start with. She soon got used to her own company again. On a weekend, Michelle would go out clubbing with her friends whilst Lisa would make up her excuses and stay in. She did some serious thinking during that time and decided that she needed some changes to happen in her life. There were plenty of things that she wanted. At the top of her list was learning to drive and buying her own set of wheels, followed closely by owning her own home. She would never amount to anything if she carried on spending all her money on drinking and clubbing. Lisa needed to start to do some serious saving and her savings book showed the grand total of ten pounds exactly, she had a lot of work to do.

Michelle continued with the clubbing scene, when getting home in the early hours she would do so quietly so as not to waken Lisa. Who would in return show equal respect, getting up quietly on Saturdays and Sundays, so as not to disturb Michelle. It worked well and Michelle was always there for Lisa to talk to if she needed her and vice versa.

Weeks went by and Michelle got to a stage where she did not go out as much either. They would either watch a film together or Michelle would be in her room reading whilst Lisa would be in hers. The clubbing scene was now nearly out of their systems, the atmosphere in the house was most definitely quieter than the earlier days when they first moved in.

Michelle was out visiting her family one evening whilst Lisa was at home alone relaxing in her bedroom. Feeling a little hungry, she decided that she would go downstairs to the kitchen to make herself a cheese and ham sandwich, her favourite sandwich filling, with a little bit of pickle. Reaching the top of the stairs, she was met by a black shadow, a very tall, broad, human shaped figure. It was so big that it literally filled the top of the stairway. Lisa could not get past it and was certainly not going to try and make any attempts to walk through it. It was as though it wanted Lisa to see it. The shadow figure kept perfectly still whilst Lisa was physically unable to move. She did not feel frightened, just a feeling of numbness along with a feeling that she should know who or what it was. It was most definitely real, she was not going to wake up from a dream. There was complete silence only interrupted by the sound of Lisa's breathing. The shadow slowly faded away until it was no more. Lisa stood there for a few moments longer trying to work out what had just happened. Part of her wanted it to reappear; she wanted to know what it was, why it wanted her to see it and what it wanted with her. No longer feeling hungry, Lisa turned around and went back to her bedroom.

Michelle arrived home, literally falling through the front door in fits of laughter, with one of her cousins, Siobhan. She was a big girl with a mouth to match. Both were wearing their sunglasses even though there was no longer any daylight left outside.

Lisa went downstairs to introduce herself and to see what all the commotion was about. Michelle looked up the staircase as Lisa was walking down and smiled. Lisa smiled in return.

"This is Siobhan, my cousin." Michelle looked up the stairs at Lisa whilst pointing her finger into her cousin's face. "She's got a bit of a fat gob on her, but she's harmless enough once you get to know her."

"Hi Siobhan." Lisa thought it only right to use her manners even if the other person did not appear to have any.

Flopping down into the chair, Siobhan said. "Michelle, make me and Lisa a cup of tea will you love? There's a good girl."

"What did your last slave die of? Make your own tea you lazy moo." Michelle not quite finishing her sentence without bursting into laughter.

"Go on Michelle love, we really need a cuppa, don't we Lisa?" Siobhan looked over at Lisa, giving her a wink. "You want a cuppa, don't you? Tell this lazy mare will you."

"Only if you're making one Michelle," Lisa said, her politeness sounding uncomfortably out of place.

"Where did you find this one Michelle?" Getting up from the chair, Siobhan started to laugh, following Michelle into the kitchen to help with the drinks.

Feeling a little uncomfortable in her own home, Lisa sat down and waited for her drink. She listened to them giggling in the kitchen and carrying on like a pair of little girls who had been allowed to stay up way after their bedtime.

Siobhan walked back into the room with Lisa's drink, Michelle following close behind. Handing a cup of tea over to Lisa, Siobhan held the cup part so that Lisa could get hold of the handle. "There you go Lisa, get that down your neck lass."

"Thank you." Lisa smiled, thinking that maybe she should not judge people on first impressions.

Michelle and Siobhan sat down at either side of Lisa, sitting on the edge of the sofa they watched her intensely as she drank her tea, not taking their eyes off her for a moment until she had finished every drop. Sitting back, they continued chatting about random things and then giggling.

Silence followed for a short while.

Siobhan looked intensely at Lisa, as though studying her, before saying, "It hasn't worked, nothing's happening."

Michelle obviously knew what Siobhan was talking about. "Give it time, you said it doesn't work the same on everybody."

Putting her hand in front of Lisa's face Siobhan started to wave it. Lisa now confused, frowned at the two of them. "What are you two talking about?"

"What do you see when I do this?" Siobhan said, still waving her hand in front of Lisa's face.

"You waving your hand in front of my face." Lisa was on the ball and ready for the next complicated question.

Michelle reached up to take off her sunglasses, putting the glasses down Lisa noticed that she looked oddly different, her pupils were like saucers where her irises had totally vanished, giving her an evil appearance. Siobhan had taken her sunglasses off, her pupils looked exactly the same, although one of her eyes seemed a lot bigger than the other one. She had never set eyes on Siobhan before so was not sure if that was what she normally looked like and thought it far too rude to make any enquiries.

Lisa's gut instincts made her feel suspicious. "You two are up to something. Have you put something into my drink?"

Siobhan appeared disappointed. "What does it matter, it hasn't even worked."

"It was an LSD tab," Michelle said, bluntly, smiling over at Lisa.

Feeling violated but strangely calm Lisa never responded, she was too transfixed with looking at them. They appeared to have turned into animals. Tipping her head slightly to one side, she stared at them both whilst examining them more closely. Siobhan reminded her of a pig with her little upturned nose, a big fat pig that was wearing an untidy peroxide wig. Whilst Michelle reminded her of one of those cute little monkeys with the big eyes that always looked so innocent and vulnerable.

Waving her own hand in front of her face she noticed that she was getting a strobing effect, she continued by standing up and waving her arms about. "Wow, I feel bloody amazing," Lisa said continuing with her strange dance routine.

Michelle looked over at Siobhan. "It's worked."

Siobhan reached into her bag and pulled out a compact disc, rushing over to the player she put it in. It was a compilation of dance music.

Like an excited schoolgirl she then rushed over to the kitchen sink, pouring lots of washing up liquid into the bowl. Turning on the hot water tap, she swished her hand about in the bowl. Michelle and Lisa followed her and watched her curiously.

"You've just got to watch the bubbles, they're amazing. Look at all the different colours." Siobhan, Michelle and Lisa stood at the side of the sink, looking down into the bowl, in a trance like state, tripping on their own imaginations. It was only stopped when Lisa developed an itch on her cheek, which she could not get to stop. The harder and faster she scratched the more intense the itch began to feel. Michelle had heard the scratching noises, turned around and grabbed Lisa's hand, managing to pull it away from her face before she scratched down to the bone. She had broken through the skin and was gradually working her way through the layers of flesh, luckily the wound would not leave a permanent scar. Lisa looked down at her nails, noticing that there was blood underneath them and all over her hand, she started to lose control and panicked.

Michelle grabbed Lisa by her shoulders and looked her straight in the eye, trying to console her, she said, "Don't worry Lisa, it's not as bad as you think it is. We'll get you cleaned up and then we'll go out for a walk." Michelle brushed Lisa's hair back from her face with her fingers. "Okay?"

Lisa took a deep breath and gave out a long sigh, "Okay."

After cleaning Lisa's hands and face, which also required a large plaster, all three of them went out for that walk. It was not long before they stopped at a field.

"Follow me," Siobhan said excitedly, running ahead with a hop, skip and a jump.

Lying in the middle of the field on their backs, arms out to the side of them, they looked up to the stars.

"Holy shit." Lisa could no longer feel the discomfort from her cheek. "I'm flying."

Siobhan and Michelle looked at each other and laughed along with her.

With no idea of what the time was or how long they had been lying in that field, they arrived back home feeling thirsty. Siobhan went over to the fridge and got out a carton of pure orange juice, which she had brought with her. Getting three glasses from the cupboard, she poured them each a drink.

"Drink this, you two." Siobhan handed them a glass each. "It's full of vitamin C which will help your coming down a bit easier and quicker."

"Coming down?" Lisa looked puzzled, having no idea what Siobhan was talking about and was not really clued up on drug taking terminology.

"Yes, it can be quite a bumpy road," Siobhan said proudly with obvious professionalism.

Putting her arm around Lisa's shoulder, Michelle gave her a little squeeze and said. "It's my first time too, we'll be all right together."

Desperately needing the toilet, Lisa broke free from Michelle's embrace and rushed up the stairs. Not having time to close the bathroom door behind her she only just managed to get her knickers down in time. Siobhan had for some strange reason decided to follow her, not managing to get as far as the top of the stairs, she was met by the black shadow at the top. Lisa could see it from where she was sitting on the toilet.

"What the? Michelle come and have a look at this. Tell me if you can see it too," Siobhan shouted back down the stairs with her mouth left gaping.

The shadow leapt forward as Siobhan turned back around, passing through her body, instinctively making her lose her balance. Falling backwards, she bounced uncomfortably all the way back down to the bottom of the stairs, her shoulder now looking obviously dislocated. The shadow was gone.

Siobhan laid at the bottom of the stairs in what appeared to be an uncomfortable position. "Did you see it?"

"See what? Siobhan look at the state of your shoulder. We need to get you to hospital." Michelle leaned forward and helped her get back on her feet. Sitting on the bottom stair she held her lifeless arm across her.

Washing her hands, Lisa joined the other two back downstairs.

"I'm telling you, it was a big black mass and it passed straight through me." Siobhan was still oblivious to the damage that she had done to herself. "You saw it, didn't you Lisa?"

Lisa sat on the stairs and pleaded her ignorance, "Saw what? I didn't see anything. Maybe you've had one of those bad trips you were telling us about, in more ways than one." Acting out of character and finding herself amusing, she started to laugh.

"It's not funny, it scared me half to death and my shoulder is really killing now." Giving Lisa a disapproving look Siobhan apparently found it more difficult to take verbal abuse than she did to give it out.

No longer feeling intimidated by Siobhan's dominant behaviour, Lisa confidently said, "I'll ring for a taxi and then they can take you to A&E." Lisa feeling smug, continued. "You'll be alright going on your own won't you? Michelle and I have work tomorrow, God knows what state we'll be in. We can't afford to lose our jobs."

"No, don't worry about me, I'll be fine," Siobhan said, with a hint of sarcasm in her tone.

Michelle had already left them and was curled up in a ball on her side on the living room floor with a cover over her head. After calling for a taxi, Lisa went to lay at the side of her and put another cover over her head.

The taxi arrived, the driver knocked on the door and Siobhan left.

It was gone ten the next morning when they both woke up with the sound of a fire engine speeding by with its sirens sounding, both totally forgetting to set an alarm call of some description.

Rubbing her back, Michelle looked a little worse for wear, her irises had reappeared though. "It took me ages to get off to sleep properly."

"Me too, my body just didn't want to shut down and worse still we're late for work now too. Look at the time." Lisa slowly stood up, every muscle and joint hurting. Putting her hands up, she shielded her eyes. "That light shining through that window is absolutely killing my eyes. I can literally feel them burning at the back."

Michelle stood up. Making her way to the front door she opened it, shielding her eyes from the light she noted that everybody seemed to be staring at her as they walked past.

Michelle was squinting as she looked back through towards Lisa. "Why the hell is everybody staring at me?"

"I don't know. Maybe because you look like crap." Lisa was trying to make light of an awkward situation. Giving out a half-hearted laugh in the hope that Michelle would cheer up, instead she just made herself feel foolish.

Closing the front door as gently as was possible, Michelle pulled down the blind in the living room before closing the curtains. Going over to the telephone, she rang work.

"Yes, good morning. Could you pass a message onto the lady that works in HR for me please? Thank you, could you let her know that Michelle Shaw and Lisa Parkins won't be in work today? We've been up half the night, think it's something that we ate last night… Yes, I will ring again tomorrow if we haven't improved."

Putting down the receiver, Michelle looked exhausted as her shoulders drooped and her body flopped forwards. "I'll see you in a few hours." Dragging herself up the stairs, she went into her room and collapsed onto her bed, within seconds she was back in the world of nod. Lisa followed her up the stairs, locking the front door first.

Lisa slept very deeply and peacefully that day, the best sleep that she had had in a long time. She was pleasantly awoken in the afternoon by the smell of bacon and eggs cooking, the aroma drifting up the stairs and underneath her bedroom door. Michelle was in the kitchen making herself something to eat. Lisa decided that she would have a lovely long soak in the bath before she went down to join her and make herself some food.

Make-up free and with wet hair tied up, Lisa burst into the kitchen and greeted Michelle, "Good afternoon and how are you on this very fine day?"

"I'm good thanks and how are you?" Michelle, looking one hundred percent better than she had earlier, putting her arms around Lisa she gave her a hug.

"Feeling good and quite surprisingly refreshed actually." Lisa returned the hug. "Don't know if it was the sleep or the bath."

"There is some bacon left under the grill if you fancy a bacon sandwich?" Michelle reached up to get a plate from the cupboard before Lisa had even had chance to answer.

"Yes please, that would be lovely. I've woken up starving."

Michelle looked sheepish like she was going to make an announcement. "I forgot to mention with all the excitement and goings on yesterday. I bumped into an old boyfriend on my way to Siobhan's yesterday."

"Did you?" Lisa said. "Have you heard from Siobhan by the way? Do we know if she even managed to make it to the hospital?"

"Oh she'll be alright, she's a tough cookie that one. I'm sure she will give us a ring later," Michelle continued eagerly, "Now listen, his name is Danny."

"Okay, go on, tell me more." Lisa bit into her sandwich, waiting for Michelle to continue.

Michelle was excited, a twinkle appearing in her eye. "He is still really cute and he was with one of his friends who seemed pretty damn cute too."

"Is one bloke not enough for you then?" Lisa said, jokingly.

"Funny ha ha. His friend is called Jason and I have invited them both to come round for dinner tonight." Michelle waited for Lisa's objections.

"Oh, okay, I will make sure that I don't cramp your style. Don't worry I will get out of your way." Lisa smiled.

"What are you talking about? Jason is coming round for you silly. I've fixed you up and I promise you that you'll love him. We're going to have a double date." Michelle had taken on the decision without first talking to Lisa about it.

Lisa felt nervous. "Oh I'm not sure. I don't think I like the idea of dating someone that I've never even met."

Michelle got more and more excited whilst trying to convince Lisa. "Oh come on, please…you haven't got any other plans already have you? Don't be nervous, honestly you'll be fine. Listen, they are both in their late twenties, have got their own cars and have really good jobs. I told him about you and he's really keen to meet you."

Lisa knew that she would not get any peace until she agreed to it. "Okay, I suppose it can't hurt. It's only dinner, after all, isn't it? What time?"

Michelle smiled, nervously. "About seven."

Washing up their plates they tidied them away before making it back up the stairs to resolve the 'what shall I wear scenario'. Most of Lisa's wardrobe contents had been removed and were now in a pile on the top of her bed. After much pondering, she finally decided on a pair of black skinny fit jeans and a plain white T-shirt, concluding that Jason could take her as he found her.

Michelle had long since chosen her outfit, a beautiful silky green dress and was already preparing dinner for them all, good old spicy meatballs and pasta followed by a lemon meringue pie. Yet more recipes from Lisa's faithful recipe book, the best four pounds and ninety-nine pence that she had spent in her life. Whilst Michelle was in the kitchen Lisa did a bit of cleaning, not wanting to let Michelle down she wanted to make a good first impression.

Danny and Jason made an appearance at exactly seven with a loud knock on the front door. Michelle, not wanting to appear too keen, answered the door after they had knocked for a second time and invited them both in whilst Lisa chuckled at Michelle's goings on. Stifling her chuckle, she was pleasantly surprised, thinking that Michelle would have kept the better looking one of the two for herself. Both were good looking and well-groomed with it. The evening was going well with plenty of laughter and chatting over dinner. Danny and Jason asked lots of questions, wanting to know more about what Lisa and Michelle did and told them about their line of work. Questions bounced around about favourite food and what music everybody liked to listen to with no awkward moments of silence. Everyone thought that dinner was lovely and complimented the chef.

It was not too long after they had finished eating that Michelle dragged Danny by his arm, up to her bedroom, not that he put up any resistance. Michelle never had been backwards at being forward and the noises that were coming out of her bedroom did not leave much to the imagination.

Lisa feeling both awkward and embarrassed thought it best to occupy herself. Standing up she started to clear the table. "I'll just clear the table and do the washing-up. You're more than welcome to help me if you want."

Jason was already on his feet and had put his arm around her shoulder, trying to guide her in the direction of the stairs. "Oh leave that, the dishes can wait. Come here!" Surprisingly for him his ego was about to take an unexpected tumble.

Lisa quickly leaned forward and bent down, so as to make his arm lose contact with her shoulder. "No!" Her response was sharp and straight to the point. She continued to clear the table, with a plate in each hand she headed for the kitchen.

"Why not?" Jason followed her, genuinely seeming confused as to why Lisa had turned down his advances.

"I don't want to. I don't even know you. I've only just met you." Lisa put down the plates on the kitchen worktop and started to walk back to continue clearing away.

Standing in front of her, Jason put his hands on her shoulders, he looked her straight in the eyes. "Yes you do. I told you plenty about myself over dinner!" Smiling, he thought it would help his cause if he turned on the charm.

Lisa returned the direct eye contact and was adamant in her response. "No, thank you."

Taking his hands from her shoulders, his smile quickly turned to a snarl. "Prick tease!"

Lisa, astonished by his reaction, remained still whilst watching him put on his shoes and jacket. Feelings of confusion came over her, she felt hurt that a man she had only known a couple of hours expected her just to sleep with him on their first meeting. Lisa was still a virgin and wanted to save herself until that special someone came along. The front door slammed shut behind him.

Continuing with clearing the table and washing-up, she tried to put the whole incident out of her head whilst at the same time trying not to listen to the entertainment upstairs. She sang along to the tunes from the radio in the kitchen before deciding to watch some television, after having had a debate with herself about if she should go out or stay in.

A flushed Michelle and Danny emerged. Danny still pulling up the zip on his trousers whilst Michelle beamed from ear to ear.

Michelle scanned the room. "Where's Jason hiding?"

Lisa, aiming the remote at the television turned down the volume. "Don't know. He decided to leave some time ago."

"Oh no Lisa, didn't it work out?" Michelle seeming genuinely concerned.

"It would appear not. I don't think I was his type of girl," Lisa said, sarcastically.

Danny was already near the front door putting on his shoes and jacket. "Thanks for a lovely evening ladies. I'd better go find him!"

"Ring me," Michelle shouted, as the front door slammed behind him.

"Are you okay? I'm sure he'll ring you."

Her forced smile showed her obvious disappointment.

Michelle was quiet for the next few days until Danny eventually telephoned her, managing to change her whole persona straight away. "We're going to the cinema on Friday, come along too if you want Lisa."

Lisa, surprised by the invitation, smiled and gave a doubtful expression, "Thanks for the invite but I'll have to decline, two's company, three's a crowd and all that."

Michelle and Danny began dating regularly. Michelle was loved up and Lisa was really happy for her with the added bonus of having the house to herself. Jason had informed Danny that he was wasting his time with Lisa, she was most definitely not his type and did not want to see her again. Needless to say, that she was not really concerned with that bit of news.

Lisa had booked a day off work to catch up with some household chores and to tackle an oversized pile of her laundry when, out of the blue, Danny called round. Lisa was at home by herself so answered the door.

"Hi, Danny. I'm sorry but Michelle's not in, she's at work all day today." Lisa stood patiently waiting to see why he had called round, she was sure that he was aware that she would not be in.

"That's okay, it's you I've come to see. I just needed to see you without Michelle being around."

Lisa could sense an air of tension and tried to lighten the atmosphere. "Oh what is it? Sounds serious! Are you planning a surprise and need my expert advice?"

Not answering, he continued to stand there staring with a serious expression on his face.

"You'd better come in Danny. Can I get you a drink?" Lisa, feeling puzzled, walked through towards the kitchen, turning around to wait for his response Danny was following close behind. "How did you know that I wasn't in work today?"

"Michelle mentioned something the other day." His behaviour was oddly very different to the man she had originally met several weeks earlier. "You do know that it's you that I want Lisa, don't you?"

Lisa coughed nervously. "Pardon, can you repeat that because I think I misheard you?"

"It's you I have feelings for Lisa, not Michelle. I had to carry on seeing her so that I could somehow get closer to you." Danny seemed convinced that his actions had been acceptable.

"I'm sorry, Danny, you're starting to make me feel really awkward. Do you know how wrong that sounds? I'm going to have to ask you to leave. Let's just pretend that none of this happened. I won't mention anything to Michelle." Lisa felt repulsed.

"Don't be scared Lisa!" Danny moved really close, putting his arm around her. "I know you want me too. I've seen the way that you look at me."

"What the hell is wrong with you? I can assure you that I have no feelings like that at all for you. You've got it all wrong. I don't know where you've got that idea from. It's all in your head," Lisa said, cringing.

She tried to push Danny away, he was obviously a lot stronger than her. He started to kiss her neck and face, putting his hand down the front of her top and started to grope her breast.

Lisa froze for a split second, her eyes widening. Without any further hesitation, she jumped backwards. "Get off me." Lisa felt panicked, wishing that someone would appear to help her.

He had already started to move towards her again, the expression on his face made it evident that he was not going to take no for an answer. Without thinking, Lisa's reactions kicked in, reaching for the nearest thing she could find, the recipe book. Hitting him as hard as she could with it at the side of his head, he lost his balance and fell over. Managing to get back onto his feet, he regained his balance.

To say that he was furious was an understatement. "You fucking little bitch."

Whilst Danny reached forward to grab Lisa, he was stopped dead in his tracks. Standing upright, like a soldier on parade, a vacant expression replaced the anger. Losing any hint of colour, his complexion became a pale ashen colour with a hint of grey, dark circular shadows appeared around his eyes which also gave a glazed over appearance. The transformation happened within seconds. Lisa watched on as he turned around and walked towards the front door. A number of small wispy black shadows had appeared just above the floor near his feet, not shadowing any definite object and each appearing to have a life of their own. Danny left calmly, saying nothing more and closed the door gently behind him. All was calm and peaceful again.

Lisa sat there for what seemed like an eternity, still in shock and feeling sick to her stomach. What had stopped Danny? What was she going to say to Michelle? Should she even say anything? Would Michelle even believe her? Should she tell the police? Was Danny going to go to the police, after all she had just assaulted him?

A few hours went by and Michelle did not get home at her usual time, Lisa had started to get even more fretful. Had Danny got to Michelle first and was she too angry to go home. Why had the police not been? Lisa was more than certain that Danny was going to attack her, even worse possibly rape her, how would she explain that to the police and to Michelle? Lisa had no evidence; it would be her word against his.

Keeping herself busy, she decided to get on with some housework, not really being able to concentrate on one job for long without moving onto another, when finally she heard the front door go. Michelle walked in looking terrible. Lisa looked at her without saying anything. She had gone over in her head, over and over again, how she was going to explain things to Michelle, but then when Lisa saw her, her mind went blank.

Looking at Lisa blankly, the words fell from Michelle's mouth. "He's dead!"

Not quite what Lisa was expecting to hear, she asked. "Did you say dead? Who's dead Michelle?"

Michelle's eyes were red and puffy where she had already done a lot of crying. "My Danny, he's dead Lisa."

"What... how the hell can he be dead?" Part of Lisa felt relieved, the other part felt sad for Michelle.

"They found him up by the reservoir in his car. It looks like he's committed suicide." Michelle started to cry again. "I just can't believe it."

Lisa who was now totally confused, was also lost for words.

"I really thought that he was the one, I love him so much Lisa. We talked about moving in together, getting married and even about having children. I wanted two but he said he wanted more."

Lisa moved closer to Michelle, putting her arm around her she rubbed her shoulder with her hand, trying her best to console her.

"I must have driven him to this. He never said that there was anything wrong. We were so happy." Michelle looked Lisa straight in her eyes. "Why would he take his own life?"

Lisa was again lost for words, her head spun and was unable to shake off the feeling of guilt. She sat with Michelle whilst she continued to cry.

Lisa packed an overnight case the next morning and went to stay with Susan and her family for a couple of days, needing to make some sort of sense of what had happened. Michelle's mother went to stay with Michelle, just to make sure that she was coping and so that she was on hand if she needed anything.

Daniel Wood or Danny as he was known to his friends, had walked out of the house and to his car, a well-maintained green MG convertible. It was his pride and joy. All men had to have something that was their pride and joy in order to feel complete or so Lisa's father had always told her. He had got into the driver's seat and sat there for a moment, in a trance, a hypnotic state and really was not in the right frame of mind to be driving. Turning the key in the ignition, he started her up. Driving for about a mile, his facial expression never changed, he pulled up on a narrow lane that ran alongside the reservoir. He had been there numerous times with lots of different girls in the past so he knew that area like the back of his hand. He was reputed to be a bit of a ladies man, Michelle refused to see or believe it, always maintaining that he was different when he was with her. Lisa was not going to be the one to spoil that fantasy for Michelle.

Opening the driver's side door, he climbed out and went to open the boot. The side compartments in the boot were not obvious at first. The secret compartments were where he kept his gun and other illegal substances. It later transpired that not all his monies were from legitimate earnings. Making a half-hearted attempt he looked around to check to see if anybody was around, taking the gun out he closed the boot gently. Sitting back in the driver's seat, he loaded his gun, opened his mouth just wide enough and placed it in. Without a second thought, he pulled the trigger. There was no pause, in the blink of an eye he had taken his own life.

A little old lady who had been out walking her little Yorkshire terrier dog found the car with Danny in it. Danny's blood splattered car had sent the dog into a frenzy, it ran around in a circle, barking uncontrollably. His brains had formed a symmetrical pattern on the inside of the rear window. The lady stood at the side of the car and shouted for help. Her feeble cries were miraculously heard and answered by a young man who had been out jogging. The police had managed to trace Michelle on Danny's mobile, she was the last person who had phoned him and they got in touch with her because there were no stored numbers on his phone.

It had been a long few days and Michelle was very quiet leading up to Danny's funeral. Michelle's mother had gone back home and Lisa had returned from her sister's house. Danny's death had really taken its toll on her. She never went out to visit anyone and told people she was too busy to have visitors. Looking exhausted, she did not make much of an effort with anything. Lisa had got over her initial guilt, consoling herself that she had not encouraged him and it was not her that had pulled the trigger or even made any suggestions that he should do so.

Danny had a good turn out to his funeral, plenty of female admirers who were sobbing uncontrollably into their tissues. Lisa noticed Jason at Danny's funeral, never speaking to either Michelle or her. It was a closed coffin funeral and a few people were in denial that he had passed away, they never got to see him and say their final goodbyes.

Lisa and Michelle went out clubbing a couple of times after that but Michelle was never the same person, there would always be part of her missing. She partly blamed herself and could not get over what had happened. Lisa knew that telling Michelle what had really happened on that fateful day was not going to help anyone so that was another secret she would have to take to the grave with her. Michelle and her parents decided that it was in Michelle's best interests if she moved back home with them. A few weeks later, she was diagnosed with depression and had to be put on medication.

Lisa carried on living in the house and was just about making ends meet. Not wanting to move back in with her parents she had to make it work by tightening her belt. Continuing to not see her parents too often made Lisa feel that she got on with them better because she did not live with them and had very little contact. If she visited them too often, John seemed to think that it was an open invitation for him to belittle her in some way, either by judging her appearance or a weakness in her personality. It still hurt her feelings, never giving him any remarks back because she did not enjoy the confrontation.

Carrying on working at the factory, she saw Michelle there occasionally. She took a lot of time off because of her illness and the doctors had difficulties with balancing her medication. She had lost her bubbly personality and that spark she once had, no longer lighting up a room when she entered it.

After working there for a couple more years, Lisa decided it was time to leave when she was offered a job working in a call centre. Saying a personal goodbye to Michelle, they had been so close once but were now like strangers, losing touch all together after Lisa left. She had a lot to thank Michelle for, teaching her how to be herself and not allowing others to intimidate her.

Chapter Five

Love and Marriage

Lisa started her new job, initially spending most of her time on her own, either going for a walk or sitting in the canteen reading at break times. Her colleagues at the double glazing call centre were friendly enough but there was not much time for small talk or idle gossip when she had her ear pressed to the telephone trying to talk to potential customers for most of the day. They all hung around in their own little gangs, Lisa once again made to feel like an outsider. Each day was the same, she would arrive at the open plan office to her partitioned off desk which consisted of a huge print-out of names and telephone numbers, a script, a pen, pad and a telephone.

Lisa had been working there for several months when one Monday morning a group of new starters arrived. Every first Monday of the month about a dozen or so new enthusiastic individuals would appear, most of them not even managing to see the week out. Being promoted to telesales leader, it was one of Lisa's responsibilities to show the newbies the ropes and go through their scripts with them. If they wanted to survive, they would need to be thick-skinned and not sensitive at all. The majority of potential customers were understandably very rude, swearing before putting down their telephones. Lisa would give them advice on how to try to stick to their scripts whilst remaining calm and refraining from being rude back at them, no matter how tempting. The latter being the hardest.

Particularly noticing one man, Lisa was instantly smitten, her eyes were drawn to him as soon as he walked through the door. An air of excitement mixed in with butterflies in the pit of her stomach, not being able to remember the last time she felt like that. Feeling herself go red, she realised that he had noticed that she was staring at him but she could not stop herself, no matter how much she tried. Smiling at Lisa, he looked nervously to the floor, making his vulnerability even more appealing to her.

Approaching her, he held out his hand to introduce himself, "Hi, I'm Steven."

Lisa noticing his large masculine hands, still felt flushed when she held out her hand. "Hi, I'm Lisa." Trying to scrunch up her toes was not helping her cause at all.

Steven was twenty-three when they first met, just four years older than Lisa. He was easy on the eye and smelt lovely too, wearing an expensive musky aftershave. He towered over Lisa, who was only as tall as his shoulder at best.

Lisa rounded up her new recruits and showed them into the conference room. The room was set out so that the tables formed a u-shape, so nobody could hide at the back of the class. Opening a couple of windows to circulate some air, the lights came on automatically as they entered. Once everyone was seated and the chatter and laughter had stopped Lisa stood at the front and introduced herself explaining what the company was all about and what was expected from each one of them. Each time would be just as nerve racking as the last. All the time she found her eyes magnetised, no matter how hard she tried she kept looking over in Steven's direction. He had the most amazing big brown puppy dog eyes.

As an icebreaker exercise, each new recruit in turn had to tell the others a little bit about themselves. Lisa paying a little bit more attention when it was Steven's turn.

"Hi everyone, I'm Steven Brook. I have not worked in telesales before, so this is all very new to me. I have tried other lines of work before but they weren't for me. I'm hoping I'm on the right track now and look forward to a career in sales."

Feeling a little disappointment that he had not given anything away about himself she handed out their scripts whilst breathing in deeply through her nose as she walked behind Steven, resisting temptation to run her fingers through his soft-looking black hair. Unsure of what she was feeling, the only thing that was certain was that she had never felt like it before. Making it a little too obvious Steven blushed again. The rest of the room seemed oblivious and were too busy concentrating on the other recruits' introductions, not appearing to notice that the teacher had a crush on one her pupils.

The training session went well without any major glitches, the new team appearing keen and raring to go. Time would tell if a couple of the 'know it all's' would survive. Each session always had at least one and someone who thought that it was their job to make the rest of the group laugh.

The remainder of the day went quickly, Lisa felt drained and ready for home when Steven approached her. "Lisa, there's a few of us going out for drinks on Friday after work if you fancy it. Nothing posh, just the local. We thought it would be a good way to end the week and get to know each other a little bit better."

Feeling flattered, but not wanting to appear too keen she said, "Yes sounds good. I've got plans later on that night so I can only stay out for a couple though."

Steven smiled and raised his eyebrows. "Friday it is then."

Lisa walked home with a bit more of a spring in her step that evening. Kicking herself, she looked at her reflection in the bathroom mirror that night with a scowled expression, she gave herself a stern warning,, "I've got other plans later on that night. What plans? Who are you trying to kid? What is wrong with you girl? Get a grip, he's gorgeous, don't go scaring him away."

As the week progressed and dragged on, each day saw less new recruits attending until Steven was the only newbie left by Friday.

Leaning against Lisa's partition, Steven looked over at her. He had a twinkle in his eye. "Wow that was a hard week. I feel drained."

She had just finished her end of week progress report for the Sales Department. Putting her pen down she turned around. "You're not kidding. Well done for seeing it through. You've managed to get a few good leads for the sales team at least. Good bit of commission if they manage to do their bit." Pausing before continuing she prayed that the answer was going to be yes. "Do you think you'll be back in on Monday?"

"Yes, sure will. Surprisingly I quite enjoyed it really, once I got over the initial rejection bit, from the customers that is. I learnt a few new swear words along the way too." Steven giggled. "Anyway, are you still up for that drink or do you need to get off to your other plans?"

"Mine's a lager and black. I'll just grab my bag," Lisa said, reaching underneath her desk.

The Wagon and Horses pub was only about a hundred yards up the road. It was quiet in there with just an old man propping up the bar. A serious refurbishment was needed and looked like it had not seen a paintbrush for years, with its nicotine stained interiors, complete with cigarette burns on the carpet. The lady who was serving behind the bar looked like she had been there since the original fixtures and fittings were installed.

Relaxed in each other's company, the conversation flowed easily. It had been a long time since she had been out and she realised how much she had missed it.

Steven changing the conversations direction, said, "I'm sorry to put a dampener on things Lisa but this beer is really lousy. How's your lager?"

Screwing up her nose and feeling relieved that he had brought up the subject first she put her glass down on the table. "Lousy, it tastes like it's been watered down."

Leaning forward, Steven whispered and looked around, "Explains a few things, like why it's so quiet in here."

Copying Steven, Lisa leant forward, exaggerating her mouth movements she whispered, "I really didn't want to mention it at first but it smells pretty rank in here too, you must have noticed it and we're not even sat anywhere near the toilets."

Both burst out laughing. Lisa looked more closely at Steven noticing that his face came to life even more when he laughed.

"Do you fancy going to the cinema or grabbing something to eat instead?" Lisa said, with her fingers crossed underneath the table. "My other plans can wait, to be honest they're not that important."

Not needing to be asked twice, he stood up and was already putting on his jacket by the time he gave his response. "Yes, let's find somewhere to eat first, preferably not in here and go onto the cinema after if you fancy it."

Steven was always the gentleman, paying the bill each time they went out anywhere and appearing insulted if Lisa made any suggestions about paying or even going halves. After a few weeks he started to stay over at Lisa's a couple of times a week, sleeping on the sofa to start with. He would give her monies to help her with the bills, even though Lisa had told him that she was coping just fine.

A few months passed by, Lisa had realised that it was definitely more than a crush, she had fallen in love with Steven. Never arguing, she had found her soulmate. He had become her whole world and she would ache when she was not with him. He was the first thing that she thought about when she woke in the mornings and the last thing she thought about before going to sleep. When not with him she would look forward and count down to when she would see him again.

One evening whilst they were watching the television, Steven got up, with a serious expression, to make them both a drink during the commercial break. Looking nervous whilst walking back through with a tray in his hands, which had two cups, a plate of digestive biscuits for them to share and a little black box on. Putting the tray down on the coffee table, he picked up the box and knelt down on one knee in front of Lisa.

Feeling her heart start to race with anticipation she even crossed her toes.

His vulnerable eyes appealing to Lisa's tenderness. "I know we haven't been together for long but I feel that you are my soulmate." Opening the box, it revealed a thin gold band with a single diamond. It made a statement without going overboard. "Would you make me an even happier man and do me the honour of becoming my wife?"

There was a short pause, whilst Lisa absorbed what he had asked and to check to make sure that she was not dreaming. "Yes. Yes of course I will."

Holding out her hand he put the engagement ring on her finger, it slid on perfectly. Getting to his feet, he pulled Lisa up from the chair. Hugging each other tight and kissing passionately Lisa felt a tear of happiness roll down her cheek and when it touched Steven's face it was trapped between them.

Reaching for a tissue, Lisa cleaned her smudged mascara from his cheek. Several more tissues were used for cleaning her own face and clearing her nose in an unladylike manner. Steven was now sat by her side and holding her hand tightly. "I'd like us to move into a place of our own, we could rent somewhere first and then move in together before we get married. Is that okay with you Lisa? You must tell me now if you think I'm rushing you into something that you don't want to do."

Not answering, instead she returned a huge smile. Stretching her arm out in front of her, she continued to admire her engagement ring.

Finding a lovely new house in a friendly neighbourhood where everybody looked out for each other, they married at a register office a couple of years later. It was a quiet affair where they asked a couple of work colleagues to be their witnesses. A honeymoon in the Lake District followed where they did not leave each other's side for the whole week that they were there.

On returning from their honeymoon, Lisa was promoted to deputy-manager at the call centre and work kindly paid her college fees so that she could study for a management qualification and climb further up the career ladder. Her life was on track and everything that she dreamt about had finally started to happen, falling into place.

On the cold evenings that Lisa was not going to college they would snuggle up together on the sofa, in front of the fire and catch up on what had been happening during the day, watching a bit of television before they went up to bed.

Steven's family and friends had contributed furniture to them, trying to save for a deposit on a house of their own was financially demanding.

Lisa had taken the recipe book with her to their new home, the book spine being a little worse for wear. Steven loved her cooking and baking, having numerous favourites but particularly liked her shepherd's pie and her fruit scones.

She would spend hours soaking in the bath, a row of lit candles at the side of her and a glass of red wine in her hand. It was her idea of heaven, there was no better way to relax. Steven would often throw hints at her that she should shower more, it would save them money on their water bill.

They had two spare bedrooms that were there for when family and friends wanted to stay over. Their bedroom was lovely, all cosy and warm, having a big comfy bed with a soft mattress that Lisa would sink into. Cushions scattered everywhere, matching the curtains and bedding. A deep piled carpet was soft under foot.

It was not too long before Lisa started to feel broody and longed to have a baby. The glimpse of a baby or a small item of baby clothing would make her feel like she was going to melt inside. Falling on deaf ears, she would nag and drop hints at Steven for months until he finally gave into the idea. After months of trying and not being successful, they started to drift further and further apart from each other.

Steven had started a new job, just out of town in the local council offices. It was just an administration job but he had been informed in the interview that it could progress into a management job in time. Using the excuse that he wanted promotion so he needed to put the hours in, he had started getting home late from work more and more often.

Not wanting to give up on him or the idea of them having a baby together, she tried her best to get close to him again. Arriving home from work one evening, as he walked through the door, he looked distant with the look of a man with the world on his shoulders. He was greeted by Lisa in the hallway, "I've cooked one of your favourites for dinner. It's in the oven keeping warm." She so longed for the old days when he would rush through the door and greet her with a big kiss and a tight hug.

Her cheerfulness was met with cold rejection. "Thanks but I'm not that hungry really. I might just have a shower and fall into bed." That loving kiss that he would give her when he returned home from work each night had long since gone.

Putting on her oven gloves, she got his dinner out of the oven and scraped it into the kitchen bin. Trying her best to hold back the tears they flooded out as she put the plate into the dishwater. The closeness that they had was replaced with distance, feeling like strangers.

Quickly wiping her tears away, Lisa decided to join him, getting undressed she got into her nightwear and laid in bed waiting for him to come out of the bathroom. It seemed like an eternity before the shower was turned off and she could hear him brushing his teeth before gargling with mouthwash. Lisa's mind started to imagine things, her paranoia setting in. He showered every morning, why did he sometimes need to shower at night as well? His job did not need him to over exert himself and he did not go to the gym, so he was not working up a sweat. Why was he getting home later more often and why did he sometimes act so coldly towards her?

Turning off the light it would be a short while after when the extraction fan would stop. Entering the bedroom, he climbed into his side of the bed, not looking at her instead turning on his side and looking away from her.

Putting a gentle hand on his shoulder, Lisa could feel a lump in her throat, as she held back yet more tears. "I'm sorry Steven."

His eyes were closed in an effort to sleep, an unfeeling tone to his voice. "What for?"

Moving closer, her body lovingly pressed against him. "Putting you under so much pressure about us having a baby." Resting her chin on his arm, she reached over putting her arm around him.

Not reacting to her warmth, he remained still. "It's okay. I'm just tired and need to get some sleep."

Rather than annoy him further, she laid back down, turning away from him and curled up on her side into a ball. It was some time before either of them managed to sleep instead laying there quietly.

The alarm clock's shrill noise woke Lisa the following morning. Reaching across to turn it off she noticed that Steven was already up and had been up for a while, his side of the bed being cold. Putting on her dressing gown, she went to look for him, first checking the hall. His jacket and shoes were already gone.

Work dragged that day, not being able to concentrate Lisa looked forward to getting home to Steven.

Laying down on the sofa that night she fell asleep whilst watching the television. She was awoken when she felt the sofa jolt, someone or something had kicked the end of it. Sitting bolt upright, she looked around, nobody was there.

"Steven?" Feeling the emptiness of the house, she knew that she was alone and that there would be no response.

Looking up at the clock, she noticed that it was nearly half past ten. Reaching for and checking her mobile there were no missed calls or messages! The landline had not rung or it would have woken her. Feeling the urge to contact him, but not able to, Steven had already asked her not to contact him because all his work calls and emails were monitored.

Climbing the stairs, she first went into the bathroom, cleaned her teeth and had a quick wash. Getting undressed she put on her pyjamas and climbed straight into bed. The smell of the clean bed linen always made her feel more comfortable. Her head hit the pillow and she fell straight back to sleep.

Lisa was awoken from a good night's sleep by her mobile alerting her to the fact that she had received a text message. Looking at her alarm clock, she just managed to switch it off before it went off. Steven's side of the bed had not been slept in.

Without looking, she knew that it would be from Steven. Rubbing her eyes, she tried to focus on the small screen. 'Sorry I didn't make it home last night. Stopped at Bob's. Late one at the office, wasn't sure if you had gone to bed, didn't want to wake you.' Communication had finally been received much to Lisa's frustration, as she was not able to reply to it.

During her lunch break that day, Lisa rang her doctor, after giving it a lot of consideration. She had decided that it was for the best that she should make an appointment to see if she had a problem with not being able to conceive. Ringing from the telephone in the conference room, she sat down on the big, comfy, leather chair making sure that the door was visible from the position she sat in.

After several attempts of an engaged tone and a few sighs Lisa's patience finally paid off when she managed to get through.

Clearing her throat with a slight cough, she was unsure as to why she suddenly felt so nervous. "Yes hello, would it be possible to make an appointment to see a doctor please?"

The doctor's receptionist having more of a schoolteacher's manner than of someone that just answers a telephone, with her exaggerated telephone voice. "Could I take your name?"

"Yes, it's Lisa Brook." Speaking quietly so as not to be overheard she routinely checked the door to make sure that she would not be disturbed.

"What would you like to see him about? Is it an urgent matter?"

Lisa paused before answering, taken aback by both her rudeness and intrusive manner. "It's a personal matter and something that I would rather discuss with my doctor if you don't mind." Remaining calm but puzzled by her last question, she continued. "Not sure what you mean when you ask if it is an urgent matter?"

"Is it life threatening?" came the terse response.

Wanting to answer with something witty, instead she took a deep breath and decided to sympathise with her, concluding that maybe she had been in the same job for too long and it was just time for her to find a different job. "Well no, but it's important."

As if my magic, her attitude improved. "I can fit you in to see Dr Blackthorn in a couple of days' time. Would that be suitable for you?"

"Yes that would be good, thank you," Lisa said, smiling at her down the telephone.

"So that's Thursday at 10 am," The doctor's receptionist repeated.

There had been no improvement on the home front, Steven would leave early for work each morning and would get home late most nights. Not wanting to add any further stress onto Steven's shoulders, Lisa kept the doctor's appointment to herself, deciding it was for the best that she did not tell him. She kept herself busy until her appointment, with work and chores around the home.

The doctor was running half an hour behind schedule, which was apparently quite normal according to other patients that were moaning to each other in the waiting room. Every time the receptionist put down the telephone, it would ring again, almost immediately. Every available seat had been taken and three children were sitting in the corner of the room in a play area scattering toys and books everywhere. An old man, who had forgotten what it was like to be young, was staring and scowling at them for not sitting still and making too much noise. Lisa had browsed through every available magazine and read every poster visible. After reading and looking at diagrams of various illnesses and memorising the symptoms of meningitis, the buzzer sounded and Lisa's name was called, it was finally her turn.

The receptionist looked over at Lisa and started pointing her finger in the direction of the corridor. "Lisa Brook for Dr Blackthorn." She was stern looking, even more so than she had sounded over the telephone.

Standing up, she picked up her bag clasping it in front of her and walked down the corridor. Looking for the door that had Dr Blackthorn's name plate on she knocked and waited.

"Come in." A well-spoken and gentle voice came from inside.

When entering his room she noted that he was an attractive young man who was very easy on the eye, not at all her usual type with his blond hair, blue eyes and fair complexion. Her eyes were then drawn to a silver framed picture sitting on his desk, presumably his wife who was unfortunately also very attractive. Further posters were on the walls with diagrams of various internal organs and it looked busy and cluttered but was professional at the same time.

Dr Blackthorn was sitting at his desk looking over towards her, his smile appearing as warm and caring as his voice. "Don't look so nervous. Please come in and take a seat Lisa." Holding out his hand, he gestured for her to take a seat. "How can I help you today?"

Sitting down, she composed herself and cleared her throat with a little cough. "Good morning. I'll just get straight to the point. I'm starting to get a little concerned that my husband and I are having problems conceiving. It's been quite a few months now and it is starting to get distressing."

"Okay Lisa, let's start at the beginning. I must make you aware that it does take some couples a good long while to get pregnant. There may not be any underlying problems at all and it may just be a question of time. Sometimes it's just simply that some couples try too hard. In my opinion it is too early for you to go along to see a fertility specialist." He paused, looking at Lisa he noted that she was listening intently. Giving her another one of his smiles before he continued, "I'll need to ask you a few questions although it might have been easier if you had brought your husband along with you."

Speaking quietly, she realised how apparent it was that she was on her own in possibly a one-sided situation. Her mind started to wander; it was a loud motorbike that sped past that interrupted her trance. Realising that the doctor was speaking to her she looked away from the window and began to concentrate again.

"Lisa, are you okay?" His concern apparent. "I lost you there for a moment. I hope I didn't offend you when I spoke about your husband."

Lisa realised that her top teeth were now resting in her bottom lip.

"I simply meant that sometimes it is easier to speak to both parties at the same time." Wide eyed he looked for some type of indication from Lisa. "Would you like us to continue or would you prefer to come back at a later date?"

"Sorry doctor. Yes I'm fine to continue."

"If you're sure." Pausing for a second time, he waited for Lisa to smile.

Happy with a response, even if it was only half-hearted, he continued. "Are your periods regular or irregular?"

Lisa was not sure if it was getting warmer in that room or if it was her obvious attraction to the doctor that was causing her to blush. "They're regular."

"It's getting a bit warm in here. Do you mind if I open a window?" Rising from his chair he walked over to the window and reached up.

Whilst he had his head turned away opening the window, she gave him a quick up and down look of approval. His jacket rose forcing Lisa to look at the shape of his bottom through his trousers, it was small but looked perfectly toned. His shoulders were broad and gave him a triangular physique. "No not at all. I thought it was just me."

Taking off his jacket, he put it on the back of his chair before sitting back down. The armpits of his shirt looked dampened. "Where were we? Oh yes. Do you smoke or have you ever smoked?"

Getting her mind refocused Lisa shook her head gently, "No, I haven't smoked."

He had now picked up an expensive looking pen and was starting to make notes on a pad. "How many units of alcohol do you drink in an average week?"

Noticing his badly bitten fingernails, she turned her thoughts to how boring she must sound and wondered if that was why Steven appeared to be less interested in her. "Not much really, just the occasional glass of wine."

"And you keep yourself healthy, plenty of exercise?" Dr Blackthorn seemed impressed by her answers.

"Yes, reasonably healthy, I do a lot of walking."

"I can see from your records that you're not on any prescribed medication. Do you take anything that isn't prescribed?" Dr Blackthorn said, not looking up from his notes.

"No, nothing." Lisa started to look out of the window again, noticing a group of older children who were obviously bunking off from school. Pushing and shoving each other into the road, giggling and smoking without a care in the world.

"I can also see from your records that you haven't been pregnant before. Can you tell me if there are any problems when you are having sexual intercourse?" Looking up for a brief moment to check that Lisa was still with him.

A little shake of her head and a frown were evidence of her bewilderment. "Not that I can think of."

Picking up on her confusion he rephrased his question. "Is it painful or do you get a burning sensation when you urinate?"

"No."

"Now, don't worry Lisa, those were just routine questions. I'd like to examine you if that's okay, I just want to check that there is nothing obvious, that stands out, to be a problem." Standing up he walked over to the door and opened it before pointing to another door. "If you could just go across the corridor to the examining room. Are you all right for me to examine you or would you prefer a female to do it?"

"It's fine for you to do it Dr Blackthorn. Thank you." Lisa now felt more concerned that she had wasted the doctors time rather than worrying about why she could not get pregnant.

Sitting on the bed, she waited in the examining room until Dr Blackthorn joined her. An uncomfortable looking bed with a plastic curtain around, a chair, a waste bin and a storage cabinet were in the clinical looking room, there were no posters or anything of any interest to look at. He was gentle on his feet as he entered the room. Asking her to lay on the bed and loosen her jeans, he pulled her T-shirt up slightly, rubbed his hands together vigorously and examined her belly and her pelvic area. His fingers were slightly cold as he moved them over her skin, pushing down gently at random places causing her to tense up and hold her breath.

"Everything feels to be okay Lisa. There doesn't appear to be anything obvious to worry about." He looked down at her and smiled as she lay still on the bed. "Now I've noticed from your notes that you don't appear to have had a smear test. It's a procedure that maybe a little uncomfortable but necessary. If you are in agreement, then I'm going to ask Nurse Brown to come in and she will perform the test and take a swab sample from your vagina.

Nurse Brown will also take a blood sample from you and ask you for a urine sample. If you don't hear anything from us within the next couple of weeks you can assume that everything is okay."

Feeling vulnerable but at the same time looked after, Lisa said, "Thank you doctor." A noticeable gulp followed.

"You're welcome Lisa." Sanitizing his hands before leaving the room, he shut the door carefully behind him. The blinds on the window were closed but the room appeared much darker than the doctor's office. Lisa realised how nervous she felt and was in two minds whether to just grab her bag and run.

Nurse Brown entered the room; there was no backing out now. She was a young woman who still looked like she had acne scarring on her face. Her hands were gentle as she carried out the test, making an uncomfortable situation feel slightly more relaxing. She was not one for small talk either. Lisa put back on her knickers and got dressed. The blood sample and urine test were a little less awkward to perform.

Lisa went straight back to work after her appointment, working through her lunch to make up her time. Feeling relieved that she had gone to see the doctor she knew that the following few days would be a struggle whilst waiting for her results.

Steven arrived home earlier than expected that night, appearing to be a little bit more relaxed than he had been in previous weeks, giving Lisa a smile has he walked through the door.

Lisa hugged him, welcoming him home. "Hi, how was your day at work?"

Returning her hug, he kissed her on the cheek before hanging up his coat and reaching down to unfasten the laces on his shoes. "A little less stressful. And you?"

Lisa felt relaxed once again in his presence, was the rocky patch finally over? She was not going to tell him about her appointment until she had got her results but instead blurted it out, wanting to talk to him about everything that had been happening to them over the last few weeks.

"It was okay. I went to see Dr Blackthorn this morning." Lisa waited for his response.

Not appearing to be at all phased by her response, he remained calm whilst he put his shoes neatly on the rack. Standing up straight again he looked Lisa straight in the eye. "Oh you never mentioned you were going to see the doctor. Is everything all right?" If surprised, he masked it well.

"I didn't want to bother you because you've been so busy recently but I am so worried about not being able to get pregnant. I feel like a failure and I don't want to let you down either." She felt like she might explode, wanting to release all her emotions and anxieties in one go. Longing for them to be close again, she loved him just the same if not more than when they first met.

Standing in front of her, Steven put his hands gently on her shoulders. "It's early days yet. You just need to be a little bit more patient. I bet the doctor told you that too."

Lisa looked up at him with teary eyes, knowing he did not feel the same anymore. That look had gone from his eyes, that energy for life and his passion for her. It was like he was somewhere else and did not want to return. "It's all I seem to think about nowadays, it's becoming an obsession with me and taking over my life. You do still want us to have a baby, don't you? Our own little family."

Succeeding in avoiding the question he did not answer, instead throwing a question straight back at her. "What did the doctor actually say?" He held her face in his hands, kissing her gently on the lips.

Feeling herself dwindle, Steven was her weakness. "Pretty much what you've just said. I've had some tests though, so we'll see what comes from that." Knowing that the doctor and Steven were probably both right Lisa took a deep breath and let out a sigh in agreement.

"I'm sure everything will be okay Lisa," Steven said, manoeuvring her in the direction of the stairs and gently slapping her bottom as she trod on the bottom stair. "Why don't you go and have one of your candlelit baths and I'll fetch a large glass of wine up for you. If you're lucky I'll even wash your back."

The bubbles were nearly over the sides as Lisa laid back down in the bath after Steven had lathered her back with soap. The glass of wine had made her feel relaxed and drowsy to the point that she had to stop herself from falling asleep. Listening to the birds outside the window, she could not remember the last time she felt so sedated.

It was only a few days later, during her lunch break, when Lisa checked her mobile, the receptionist at the doctors had left her a voicemail message asking her to make an appointment as soon as possible. They had found something, what was it? The doctor said that they would be in touch if there was anything wrong and it must be important if they want to see her urgently.

Fearing the worst, Lisa went into the conference room to return the call.

Perching herself on the edge of the table she did not have to wait long until the receptionist picked up her call. "Hi, it's Lisa Brook. You left a message for me on my mobile. I need to make an appointment with Dr Blackthorn as soon as possible please."

It was a younger lady, with a more charming manner about her that spoke, "Thanks for ringing back Lisa. I can fit you in this afternoon at about 4.15. Will that be convenient for you?"

"Yes. I should be able to finish work early," Lisa said. "Can you tell me, is it something serious?"

"I don't know, doctors don't divulge patient's cases to us. I was just asked to contact you," The doctor's receptionist said feeling obviously powerless.

Lisa's life turned on its head with that visit. Sitting in the doctor's waiting room listening to her own breathing, she knew that something was wrong. Had they found something life threatening? She sat and waited for the worst, how long did she have left to live?

Baffled by how she was sitting in Dr Blackthorn's office, not able to remember the receptionist calling out her name or walking down the corridor she listened to him only half hearing what was being explained to her. "The smear test results are not yet available, they should be with you within the next few days and you should receive them in the post. Your blood tests have confirmed that you are immune against rubella and varicella." Dr Blackthorn paused, looking at Lisa with a more serious expression, he continued. "Now, Lisa, the swab test and urine test have both come back reading positive, you have contracted chlamydia."

Feeling ignorant, she looked at the doctor for reassurance, unsure if she should feel relieved or terrified. Was it a common illness that a lot of people developed or was it a rare disease that only about one in a million got? "Sorry, doctor, I've not heard of it before. What is it?"

"It's a sexually transmitted infection. You can have it for a long time and not show any symptoms whatsoever. But if it is left untreated it can cause lots of problems, including infertility." Dr Blackthorn scribbled something on his prescription pad. "I'm going to put you on a course of strong antibiotics. Do not drink alcohol while you are taking them or they will become ineffective. You will need to come back in about three months' time, so that we can check to make sure that the antibiotics have worked. I know that you are trying for a baby but if you could please have protected sex until we give you the all clear."

Lisa made it apparent that she was equally confused and annoyed. "It's just not possible doctor. I think that there has been some sort of mistake, maybe a mix up with my results. I can assure you that I do not sleep about, Steven is the only person I have ever slept with. I know that he had a few sexual partners before we got together but he told me that he had been checked at a clinic before we slept together and he was given the all clear." Looking at the doctor, she so wanted him to own up to his mistake and apologise, deep down she knew that she would have a long wait.

The doctor's response was firm, "Lisa you definitely have chlamydia and there has been no mistake or mix up. Although the damage to men is not as bad as it can be for women you will still need to tell your husband as soon as possible so that he can get the treatment that he needs too."

Tearing the prescription from the pad, he handed it to Lisa. "You need to start taking these as soon as you can."

Her head spun whilst her stomach churned. Feeling stupid for being rude, she smiled at him as a way of an apology. "Thank you doctor."

Returning her smile, he nodded his head. "I'll see you soon and take care Lisa."

Feeling bruised when she arrived home, she picked up the post from the hallway mat. Walking through into the kitchen she threw it straight down onto the worktop without first looking through, where she would normally have put any junk mail straight into the bin. Filling the kettle, she made herself a cup of tea and sat on the kitchen chair staring out of the window. Not thinking of any one thing in particular, she tried to remain calm and not get herself worked up.

Still sitting on the chair with her shoes and coat on when Steven arrived home from work, he had graced her with his presence a little earlier than usual again that evening. Not moving she listened to him close the door behind him, pictured him taking off his jacket and shoes in his usual manner and listened to him as he shouted to her whilst walking up the stairs.

"Lisa, I'm just going to go and have a quick shower before dinner." Not waiting for a response, he continued with little regard to checking if she was actually home or questioning how she was or how her day had been.

From the bottom of the stairs, she could hear that the shower was running. She reached into the pockets of his jacket, fumbling about until she found his mobile phone. Pulling it from his breast pocket, it pinged to reveal a new text message had arrived from someone called Olivia. The name did not ring a bell, he had never mentioned anything about an Olivia. Not opening the text, she thumbed through and noted that most of the messages on his phone were from the same Olivia.

Lisa's curiosity got the better of her as she opened the text. It read, 'Hi S, sorry I couldn't make our rendezvous this evening. Had to get home to Mark, you know what he's like. Love you darling. Xxx'

Her stomach bile rose into her throat as she stopped herself from vomiting. Not having time to put the phone back in his pocket, Lisa heard the stairs creak. Without looking up she knew that Steven was there. She had been caught red-handed. His face did not seem concerned, he appeared to be more relieved than anything.

Lisa was the first to speak, as she felt unsure as to why she looked like the guilty party. "Thought you were having a shower."

"I was just going to get my phone." He stood there with his dressing gown around him.

Wasting no time, Lisa got straight to the point. "Do you love her Steven?"

Without responding, Steven turned around and walked back upstairs, went into the bathroom and turned off the shower before returning to join Lisa in the kitchen. Sitting back on the same chair, Steven's phone was on the worktop with the latest text message visible.

"Do you love her, this Olivia, whoever she is?" Lisa said, not allowing herself to get tearful, all she wanted was some honesty. Feeling strong, she was not going to allow him to carry on behind her back. "Please Steven, just answer my question. I'm asking you nicely. I promise that I won't kick off or anything. You owe me that much at least."

To Lisa's surprise, Steven's eyes were filled with tears. "Yes I do. But I love you too."

Lisa, unsure of where the questioning was going, continued. The words appeared to come out of her mouth without much thought behind them. "How long has it been going on?"

Steven felt cornered and looked down towards the floor. "Not long."

She knew he was lying and was not happy about being treat like a fool. Her voice rose as she could feel the spark of anger inside her igniting. "How long Steven?"

Sitting down on the kitchen floor, he leant his back against the cabinets, his legs outstretched in front of him. "I've been seeing her off and on for about five years." His eyes filled with panic as he realised just how deceitful it all actually sounded.

"Five years." Lisa was stunned, continuing, she wanted to put more of the pieces of the jigsaw puzzle together. "Steven, I'm really confused now because that's longer than we've been together. So who the hell is she then?"

"I met her at work as well, she's the receptionist at a company I used to work at." Putting his knees up, he started to act like a small child as he hugged them in a protective manner.

Her attention was side-tracked whilst listening to the rain lashing against the window with some force. Feeling a cold breeze, it caused the hairs on her arms and on the back of her neck to stand up. "Why did you bother with me if you were already seeing someone else? And don't you think that it would have been nice if you had actually told me that you weren't available?"

Standing up he went to look outside the window. "It wasn't that simple."

Looking at his reflection in the window, she continued. "Really. Why? Seems simple enough to me." Feeling tempted to pick something up and throw it at him, instead clasping her hands together.

Lisa could see that he was looking at her in the reflection. "Because she's married. She is an older woman who has children with him. She won't leave him because he has money and can give her things that I can't."

Getting up from her chair, she walked over to put the kettle on. "Oh I get it now. You're with me because you can't have her. You're stuck with me instead."

He was now standing behind her, putting his arms around her waist he kissed her on the back of her neck. "I'm not stuck with you. Don't you get it Lisa? I love you."

Moving her head away, she turned back around and pushed him away from her whilst smiling sarcastically. "I went back to the doctor's today, you know for my results. Apparently I've got an STI, which you have very kindly given to me."

Taking a step backwards, Steven appeared to be more shocked than Lisa on hearing the news. "An STI. What STI?"

"Chlamydia. So you need to see your doctor too." Not sure if to feel sorry for him or laugh at his shocked facial expression, she ironically said. "Please remember to give Olivia a personal thank you from me."

"Are you sure that it's something that I have given to you?" Steven asked with all sincerity.

Lisa's adrenaline level was overflowing as she started to cry. "You really are unbelievable, you cheeky bastard. How dare you?"

"I'm so sorry Lisa. You were never supposed to find out. I didn't mean to hurt you." Steven reached out to Lisa. "You've got to believe me. Where do we go from here?"

Resting her head against his chest he put his arms around her, holding her tight. Despite everything she still loved him. "I don't know. I don't know about anything any more. Our relationship has been based on one big fat lie. You've lied to me from the beginning and I don't mind admitting to you that I hurt. You've ripped my heart right out of my chest and I don't know if I will heal."

Kissing her gently on the top of her head, Steven said, "Please give me a chance. We could start again, Lisa."

Lisa looked up to him, her eyes bloodshot and tired. "I really don't know, I need time to think. What about Olivia? Every time you're not with me or you're late I'll be thinking that you're with her. I had to check your phone tonight, I've never felt the need to do that before today."

Holding her at arm's length he held the tops of her arms. Realising that he had been foolish his eyes were filled with warmth. "I'll end it with her. I promise."

Turning her back to him she put a teabag into her cup before pouring the hot water out of the kettle. "Just go and have your shower, Steven."

She could smell his sweet breath as he stood right behind her again. "Will you still be here when I come back down?"

Scooping the bag out of the cup with a teaspoon, she walked over to the fridge to get out the milk. "Yes, I'll still be here. I've not got anywhere else to go have I?"

Tensions were high in the Brook household, a mixture of betrayal and hurt. They carried on living separate lives under the same roof for a few weeks after the confession. Steven managed to get home early for a couple of weeks but it was not long until he started to arrive home later again. Feeling disappointment Lisa never questioned him, she knew he was betraying her again, the smell of Olivia's perfume on him was too strong to mask.

Sitting at the kitchen table one evening, the local evening paper open, half-heartedly looking at properties to rent and wondering if it should be her that left or Steven when he popped his head around the door to announce that he was going out. "I'm just going down to the Duck and Drake for a couple." It was their local pub and somewhere that they had gone quite a lot when they first got together. Part of her wanted to jump up and go with him, reminisce about old times and try to ignite that old spark but she knew deep down that it was over between them.

"Okay." Glancing up at him as he was going out of the door she noted that he looked very pale, dark around his eyes and they were glazed over. She had a strong feeling of déja vu. Standing up so that she could see the floor around his feet she knew that there would be the small dark shadows. His fate was now out of her hands. Feeling a little scared when she went up to bed that night, she knew that she would not see Steven alive again.

Steven had been on his way to the Duck and Drake pub. Walking down the path he headed towards the bridge, the grass was now overgrown at the sides and the odd nettle stung him through his trousers, not that he appeared to notice.

The river under the bridge was flowing fast, it always did after a really heavy rainfall. Floating along the river there was the odd large branch and a few little twigs which the wind had brought down.

It was an old metal structured bridge with concrete slabs and had stood the test of time through many rough winters. He was in a trance like state when he stepped on to the bridge. Climbing carefully up onto the top hand rail he managed to balance there for a few seconds. Putting his arms out to the sides of him whilst looking straight ahead, he fell forward, hovering in the air like a bird waiting to attack its prey, before falling down into the river. The only noise made was when his belly hit the water, flat. He had always been a good swimmer but he made no effort to save himself as he surrendered himself to the strong current of the water, voluntarily putting his face underneath.

Upsetting but it came as no shock to Lisa when the police managed to find Steven's body a couple of days later, after reporting him missing only the day before.

Lisa received a letter from Steven's solicitor a couple of weeks after the funeral explaining that he had a will in place. She had been left all of his belongings, which included a life insurance policy. It was a nice tidy sum, which she had no prior knowledge of and she made arrangements for the monies to be paid straight into her bank account.

A few weeks later whilst sorting through Steven's belongings, to take to the charity shop, Lisa found a scratch card in the inner pocket of a suit jacket. Throwing it on the bed she didn't scratch it until later when she was making herself a light meal. After checking it numerous times, it was a definite winner, matching three amounts the same, £50,000.

Chapter Six

A Fresh Start

Progressing to management level within the call centre no longer seemed that important to Lisa, her priorities had changed over the months following Steven's demise. Almost completing her course she decided to drop out of college, it was not for her any more. She had learned plenty but felt that life was too short and wanted more from it. The loneliness she could cope with, the memories, both good and bad, at work and home were a different matter. Everywhere she looked, there would be reminders, sometimes gentle and sometimes not so. Music playing on the radio or a certain smell would trigger memories that she had long since forgotten.

After receiving the all clear from her doctor, Lisa decided that it was for the best that she start to make plans to move away. With the money that they had managed to save together, Steven's life insurance and the scratch card win Lisa managed to get her thoughts together and make a final decision.

Working her notice at work, she made visits to the Lake District each weekend, browsing through the estate agents and viewing properties. The weeks soon passed and Lisa was kept busy with house hunting, working and packing up her belongings at home ready for the move. The Lake District had always fascinated Lisa, with its beautiful scenery and peaceful surroundings. The pace of life was one where she had time to appreciate what nature had intended. Each time she had visited she felt like that was her home, where she belonged.

Not being able to sleep the night before moving day, excitement and anxiousness were Lisa's reasons for getting up early. Eating breakfast, she showered and made sure that everything was packed away before having a final clean around. Her landline had been disconnected, she had arranged for her post to be redirected and had already notified everyone that needed to know about her move and had taken final electric and gas meter readings. After having a final check of her to-do list she propped herself on the chair arm in the living room and stared out of the window, waiting for the removal men to arrive.

Lisa had found herself a lovely little one bedroom apartment and had still managed to have money left in the bank. The removal men, who looked like a modern day Laurel and Hardy, arrived punctually and took over, much to her relief. Not stopping for a rest they soon had the house emptied. Getting into their van they were on their way. Lisa stood there with little regrets, the house was now totally empty. Not only of furniture but of the life that she had shared with Steven. With mixed feelings of both sadness and excitement Lisa walked from room to room checking to make sure that nothing had been left behind, each room giving her so many unique memories, both good and bad. Closing the front door behind her for the last time she walked to the estate agents to hand in the keys.

Her train was a little delayed but the rest of the journey ran smoothly. On arriving at her new home, she noticed that the removal men had already arrived and were sitting in their van. The driver had his head resting backwards with his mouth open as he caught forty winks whilst his passenger had his feet on the dashboard reading a newspaper and eating a sandwich. Lisa signalled him with a wave of her hand to let them know that she had arrived and went straight up to the apartment to unlock the door.

The apartment was on the middle floor of five floors, was very modern and had everything she needed. She most loved the fact that she could walk about in her bare feet because of the underfloor heating. Lisa was greeted with a faint aroma of cigar smoke as she entered the apartment. Thinking it a little strange she went to open a couple of windows to let the fresh air in. When looking around the apartment initially the estate agent told her that nobody had ever lived in that particular apartment before.

The removal men finished their break and began to take the difficult, heavier items up to the apartment first. Leaving the door open Lisa went down to collect the box from the van that she had marked up 'kettle' and carried it back up. This box also contained cups, coffee, teabags and sugar. She had already called in at the shop in the train station for a pint of milk and once she had rinsed the pots out she made everyone a hot drink.

All of the furniture and boxes were now in the right rooms, all Lisa had to do was empty them and put everything in its rightful place. There were a lot of boxes and it would take some time. After paying the removal men with a cheque Lisa thanked them for all their hard work and locked the door behind them. Standing back, she smiled whilst looking around her new home. Starting on the first box she emptied out the candles, putting most of them in her bathroom. The green foliage was placed on the window bottoms throughout her new home, it made the place look more homely and not as clinical.

Emptying box after box she decided that she would continue the day after. Making her bed had become her priority. Half tempted to just lay on top of the mattress, she was tiring and putting on the duvet cover had never felt like such a chore. Laying on her bed she stared up to the ceiling, her relaxation was only interrupted by what looked like someone walking past the bedroom door out of the corner of her eye.

Sitting straight up, Lisa gently said, "Hello? Is anybody there?"

There was no response. Being used to strange unexplained happenings occurring, she was not phased when she got up from her bed and went to look to see if someone else was in the apartment with her. Inhaling deeply through her nose, again she noticed the slight smell of cigar smoke. Tiptoeing around her apartment, so as not to disturb any possible intruder, firstly she went into the living area and looked into each room in turn, the bathroom and kitchen were empty. She was alone.

Sleeping well that night she awoke to the sound of the birds twittering outside of her window. It looked like it was going to be a lovely day, just a bit of cloud cover which the sun would soon burn away. Looking out of the window, she looked below and saw people out jogging, both individually and in small groups. Dog walkers stood and looked patiently at their dogs before they cleaned up their messes.

Lisa had so looked forward to her fresh start where no one else knew her. Apart from Susan and her family, nobody else knew where Lisa had intended to move to.

The older they got, the closer Lisa felt to Susan. She had given Elizabeth her telephone number as a point of contact if she wanted to get in touch, but she was not going to hold her breath.

Firstly, she needed to get down to the local shop and buy some essential groceries, not having much to eat the previous day she had awoken feeling ravenous. Grabbing the same clothes that she wore the day before, she quickly got dressed before heading out of the door. It was still pretty early and nobody else appeared to be awake in the block. The nearest convenience store was just around the corner. It was a little pricey so she just bought herself some croissants, a jar of jam and the local newspaper which featured the job vacancies. A little exploring would need to be done later however to find a cheaper place to shop.

Unpacking and settling in quickly it was only a week into the move when Lisa had managed to secure a part-time job helping out in a local bed and breakfast, named Woodhayes. The owners were a friendly middle-aged couple called June and Barry Hayes. The bed and breakfast name came about because June's maiden name was Wood, so they combined their surnames together. Lisa worked mornings and helped with changing the beds, cleaning the rooms and helping out with any other chores as and when it was required. It was not long before June and Barry made her feel more like one of the family.

The guests that stayed at the bed and breakfast always appeared to be in good spirits and were very friendly. They were mainly well to do people who had lovely manners and several were regular guests. Lisa was allowed to keep any tips that the guests left in the rooms for herself and if the guests ever left their belongings Lisa would always hand them in at the reception.

Living in a lovely friendly village made it easy to meet lots of new people. Lisa already did quite a lot of walking but felt honoured when she was invited to join a group that went hill walking every Sunday. They would always finish the day with a Sunday dinner and a drink in the local pub, The Red Squirrel. They were in the main a lovely group and some of them always had a story to tell. Most of them were quite a bit older than Lisa but they were definitely a spritely bunch. On the first few walks she definitely had problems keeping up with them but it did not take long for her to get used to their pace.

Some of the walkers would visit the Lakes every weekend. Others only occasionally and some of the other walkers were locals. The number going on the walk depended on how many people were available, usually it varied between six and twelve. The group would meet up at the same place and at the same time, Lisa tried her best to go every week.

Derek had been visiting the Lakes since he was a child and soon after he was widowed, he had started to visit every weekend, give or take the odd occasion. He was a lovely old man and liked to tell everyone stories about his late wife, Emma, and how proud he was of his only daughter, Veronica. She was a successful surgeon who lived in New York and had been given American citizenship. Veronica did fly back to visit Derek occasionally but he could not afford the air fare to New York and would not take hand-outs from Veronica, as he called them. Missing both his wife and daughter he loved to visit the Lakes because he had such fond memories of them both there. It was his way of being close to both of them. Treating Lisa like a daughter, he was always very kind and caring to everyone else in the group too.

There was Mavis who Lisa really did not have much time for. Trying to get along with her was extremely hard work and Lisa was not the only one that felt like that. A bitter old woman who only went on the walks so she could have a good moan and to reiterate how useless the entire male population was. Even though Mavis was local luckily she was somebody who did not go with the group too often. Lisa did not really engage in conversation with her for too long, if she could help it, she had an amazing ability of making Lisa's feelings sink.

Mr Kenneth and Mrs Irene Butterworth were a delightful old couple and made Lisa feel inspired. They had been married for over fifty years and had never spent a night apart. They went everywhere together and Lisa had never heard a cross word exchanged between them. If one of them made a comment the other one agreed with it, whereas some of the couples Lisa knew tended to bicker and contradict each other at any given opportunity, just because they could. Like most couples they had experienced sorrow in their lives. Being unable to have children of their own they spoilt their many nephews and nieces instead. Lisa would sometimes feel a little sad when she thought about how devastating it would be if one of them passed away and how the other one would feel and cope. They had a beautiful kinship which one day would inevitably end in such terrible heartache.

Sally worked in the kitchen at Woodhayes Bed and Breakfast with Lisa, helping out with breakfasts and washing-up the dishes. June was insistent that the washing-up was done the old fashioned way, not with one of those silly dishwashers. Sally was a pleasant and cheerful woman in her early forties, although from stories Lisa had heard from local people, Sally was not really someone you wanted to get on the wrong side of. Her partner's name was Maxine, they had lived together for a few years but lived quite separate lives, each doing their own thing on a Sunday. Sally liked walking whereas Maxine was more of a stay in sort of person who would play on her games console.

There were two brothers, Adam and Rob, who were local lads that used to go along too. They were Mavis' nephews and were like chalk and cheese. Lisa had only found out that they were related to Mavis purely by accident when other walking group members had mentioned it to her in passing. The brothers never walked with or spoke with Mavis. Adam was the oldest by a couple of years, acting way more mature than Rob who had a cheekiness about him that was difficult to ignore, giving everybody a guided tour of everything, if they wanted it or not.

Another middle-aged couple would occasionally go along with them, keeping themselves to themselves and did not go along for Sunday lunch with them after the walks. Even though they were not talkative they always greeted everyone in the group and would smile politely. Some of the group had categorised them has being weird, Lisa preferred to think of them as just being quiet people who did not want everybody else knowing their business. The wife appeared to be very timid whilst her husband seemed to take the lead, making all the decisions by himself without first consulting her.

Lisa always looked forward to Sundays, feeling part of a community and having like-minded friends meant the world to her.

One Sunday, after finishing her lunch she drank up deciding to head off back home, feeling a little bit more tired than usual. Usually enjoying the catch-up and chatter afterwards she concluded that level of lethargy usually meant either a cold or virus would follow. The Red Squirrel was not far from her home but she still had a little walk. A dull annoying headache now joined her other symptoms and all she could think about was falling onto her bed and getting some serious sleep. It was unusually quiet in the village for a Sunday; most probably because the weather had taken a turn for the worse, the skies looked stormy.

Walking past the shops, she noticed a tall well-built man in the reflection of one of the windows and he was looking directly over at her. It had been a long while since a man had paid her any attention, especially one that was quite a bit younger than her. Walking on the path on the other side of the road he started to cross over towards her before drawing parallel with her. Feeling a little nervous she found much needed energy and picked up her pace, looking down at the ground pretending that she had not noticed him. Blocking her path, he stood right in front of her. "Excuse me love, sorry to pester you but do you have the time on you?" he asked with obvious confidence. A wisp of black hair peeked out from underneath his beany hat, which she thought made him look cute, even though he was taller than her. He had a lovely genuine friendly face which made her feel a little calmer.

Raising her arm to look at her watch, she said, "Yes of course, it's …"

Lisa did not have time to finish answering his question, quickly noticing his hand had gone into his jacket pocket. Remaining calm and controlled, he pulled out a knife, flicking it open he held the blade against Lisa's stomach. His face grew closer to hers; as if it was possible to intimidate her any more than what he had done already. "We can do this the easy way or the hard way." His head tilted to one side. "Your choice." His head tilted to the other side. "Just hand over your money or the blade goes in." His facial expression remained constant with no regards for Lisa's horror.

Left speechless she handed over her purse and its contents. Trying to be brave her eye contact remained with his whilst she could still feel the blade pressing against her. In reality she was terrified and had to stop herself from screaming for help.

Snatching it from her hand, he opened it. "Where's the rest?" Shaking her head, he rummaged about in her pockets. Feeling him touch her inappropriately, she remained still, taking deep controlled breaths. Grabbing her bag, he tipped the contents onto the floor. A small mirror cracked as it hit the floor, a lipstick rolled into the road and a couple of tampons lay there alongside her hairbrush. Throwing the bag down onto the floor he turned around and ran off with the purse. Dropping to the ground she sobbed realising at that point that she had already wet herself, at which precise moment she was unsure.

There had not been much cash in Lisa's purse, she did not carry any plastic cards with her unless she knew that she needed to visit a cashpoint, only ever taking enough money out with her that she knew she was going to need along with a small emergency surplus. She had always done that, it was mainly to stop herself from overspending and on the off chance that something like this might have happened to her.

As he ran off, he turned around briefly, looking back at Lisa. His facial expression had not changed; his complexion however looked much paler with a definite darkness around his eyes, making them look sunken. He looked so different, his cuteness had been replaced with an all too familiar death mask. Looking down at his feet she expected to see the wispy shadows, but there were none. As if behind schedule, they appeared out of the ground at the side of her, hovering as if first checking to make sure that she was all right before quickly gliding off to catch up with him.

Never feeling as scared in the whole of her life she remained seated on the ground, hidden away in a corner with her back leaning up against a wall. Her knees were tucked up against her stomach has she hugged them, not moving until she was sure that he had definitely gone. Not another soul was about to help as she got herself up from the ground before quickly running all the way back to her apartment without stopping. Getting out of her wet clothes, she threw them straight into the washing machine before taking a long hot bath.

Dripping wet and still feeling slightly shaken she put on her bathrobe, got a bottle of red from the wine rack and poured herself a large glass. Sitting at the kitchen table, she put her head into her hands and sobbed.

Lisa made her excuses that she felt too ill to go into work the following day. She really just wanted to hide away from the world, not wanting to talk to anybody about what had happened and knew that if she spent the day by herself hidden away then she would be back to her normal self in next to no time. The day seemed to drag as she laid in her bed, under the duvet, feeling sorry for herself. She did not want to lay there any more and did not want anything to eat, she had lost her appetite. Deciding to keep herself busy, she cleaned her apartment from top to bottom, even though it was already immaculate.

Managing to make herself a little bit of chicken soup and a couple of slices of toast later that evening she put her food on a tray and went into the living room. Sitting down on the settee, she pressed the remote control and started to watch the television. The local news had just started.

The female newsreader had a local accent and would appear to maintain a smile, no matter how upsetting the headline. "Coming up on tonight's news. How a bizarre death is being investigated in what appears to have been a horrific murder last night. And how a local man has raised even more money for a local hospice and what we can expect from the weather in the coming week."

Intrigued Lisa continued to watch whilst putting a spoonful of soup in her mouth. Taking the spoon back out again with the hot soup still on, she blew onto it to cool it down before slurping. A photograph of the man who mugged her yesterday appeared to fill the screen. Closing her eyes, she reopened them looking at the picture again before making a large gulping noise as she swallowed her food.

Leaning forward she put the tray onto the floor, sitting on the edge of her seat she continued to listen with more interest. "Whilst the Mountain Rescue team were coming back from a routine training exercise last night they noticed something out of the ordinary. Because of the nature of the incident we have been asked not to show any photographs or films at this time." Amazingly the newsreader's smile no longer remained, instead she looked disturbed. "It is believed that the man's name is Jack Lowe and he is not local to the area. His next of kin has been notified. The young man was found hanging naked upside down with serious fatal injuries to his body. A nearby smouldering fire had fragments of clothing, believed to be that of the man. The police are making further investigations. If anybody knows this man or saw anything suspicious then crime stoppers are asking if you can get in touch with them. A telephone number can be seen at the bottom of the screen."

Lisa turned off the television, picked up the tray, walked into the kitchen and put it on the worktop before residing back to her bedroom. Curling up on top of her bed she looked over in the direction of her bedside cabinet. The purse that Jack had robbed from her was on the top of it. Picking it up, she unzipped it, to find that the money was still inside.

Jack had stopped running once he was out of Lisa's sight. Placing her purse carefully inside his jeans' pockets he started to walk. As if programmed like a robot he changed his direction, turning he walked towards the hills. Still on his own, he was not suitably dressed to go walking. It was not long until he was out of the village and making his way up into the hills. Picking up momentum, he started to run, not really out of breath until he nearly reached the top. Remaining focused, he paid no attention to his surroundings. Slipping a few times, he managed to pick himself up and carry on running, collecting a few cuts and bruises on his knees and his shins on his way up.

Coming out of his trance, he sat down on a boulder, bewildered as to how he had got there. He was finding it hard to catch his breath, concentrating hard he took deep breaths and tried to remain calm.

Trying to stand up he found that he was not able to move. Looking down at his hands he got the strangest sensation that his arms did not belong to him as a black mist started to leave his body. He was again able to move but the mist had started to take on human form.

"What the fuck!" Jack said out loud, trying to scramble backwards.

Leaning forward the shape slowly positioned its head right in front of Jack's face. The black shadow started to speak to him. "We can do this the easy way or the hard way. Your choice. Just hand over the purse or the blade goes in."

Jack's eyes widened. The entity could sense his fear and fed from it. Taking Lisa's purse from his pocket Jack placed it at the side of him.

Almost touching Jack, it remained close. "Stand up and take off your belt."

Standing up, the black shadow rose at the same time right in front of him, mirroring his every move. Taking off his belt, Jack dropped it to the ground at the side of him. He was no longer under its spell; instead, he had voluntarily decided to follow its orders.

"Take the knife out of your pocket slowly and put it on the ground," the black shadow said, calmly.

Putting his hand into his pocket Jack took out the knife but instead of putting it on the ground, he flicked it open and rushed at the entity, taking a jab at it. The entity roared with thunderous laughter as Jack fell through it. Falling onto a rocky outcrop the entity entered Jack's body before he had chance to hit the ground and levitated him back up onto a ledge.

It was now in front of Jack again, not quite as close this time but enough to make him feel uneasy. "Even though you amuse me, I'm not in the mood for your silly games. Now be a good chap and put the knife onto the ground." The entity floated above him, lowering itself to either side of him before stopping and remaining still behind. "You do know that you are going to die, don't you? I'm going to enjoy killing you and the more you try to resist, the harder it will be for you."

Jack doing as he was told this time, placed the knife on the ground to the side of him. An uncomfortable silence followed. The weather had definitely taken a turn for the worse. A fine rain had started which was soaking through to his skin whilst the gentle breeze had picked up strength, causing the hairs on his arms to stand up on end.

Twisting his body, Jack tried to turn around to look behind him, the wind blowing into his eyes, causing them to water. Not able to focus on the entity he nervously started to question its motives. "Who are you? More to the point, what are you? And what the hell do you want with me?"

The entity remained quiet for a moment longer before giving its response. "Take off your clothes, Jack."

Jack started to undress. Stalling for time, he folded and placed his clothes in a tidy pile on the wet ground. "How do you know my name?"

The black shadow put his head slightly to one side as he watched Jack undress. Jack's underwear had recently been soiled.

Jack could feel a force push down on his shoulders. "Sit down Jack."

His once arrogance had been replaced with dread. "Please just tell me what are you going to do to me?"

The entity had grown bored, wanting to complete its duty and get on its way. "Silence, Jack. No more questions. No more talking."

Gulping, Jack's breathing became louder and erratic.

Feeding from Jack's anxiety, the entity continued. "Put the belt around your ankles and pull it as tight as possible."

Jack froze for a split second before picking up his belt. He had contemplated running, but where would he go? Instead, he hoped that whatever it was that was tormenting him would just disappear and change its mind. Putting the belt around his ankles, he fastened it before letting it go. The belt tightened with an unbearable grip and Jack let out a scream. His feet were hoisted into the air, followed by his legs until Jack was hanging upside down. A loud bang could be heard as a nail was put through the belt and into the rocky outcrop. The entity hovered upside down in front of him, roaring with laughter.

The entity slowly disappeared until it was no longer visible and there was complete silence. Jack reached up and tried to reach his belt to untie it, but the more he moved the more the belt tightened, making the pain worsen.

"Help." Jack's face had turned red as he screamed, the veins sticking out and pulsating against his temples. "For fuck sake will someone please help me?" His cries for help could not be heard. Closing his eyes, he breathed out heavily, giving out a loud sigh. When inhaling again he could smell burning and could see smoke drifting in front of him.

It was only then that Jack noticed through the smoke that his flick knife was hovering in front of him at waist level. Putting out his hand, he waved it in front of him trying to knock it out of the way. Without any notice the knife lunged forward, jabbing him through the back of his hand and pulling straight back out again. Darting forward it stabbed him just above his hip, neatly slicing him straight across his lower abdomen to his other hip. Jack's body now hung lifelessly, his intestines peeking through the gash. Pressure and gravity taking over they spewed out, hanging over his face and blanketing the ground below. The entity was gone.

Lisa had not been to the police and reported the mugging and now had definitely had no intentions of doing so.

The next day Lisa went into work, trying to act as normal as she possibly could, keeping her head down, speaking when spoken to and smiling at the right times. The guests and her colleagues were still talking about the murder, Lisa did not engage in the conversations. It was the talk of the entire village, nothing like that ever happened there.

Lisa went straight home after work, locking and bolting the door behind her.

Chapter Seven

William Oates

The Stuart Morton School of Motoring car pulled up on the street below Lisa's apartment. It stood out from all the other cars with its obvious illuminous lime green colour and all its signage. Stuart, who was Lisa's third driving teacher, was always punctual and would park up in the exact same place every week without fail, never letting her down. Previous teachers had failed her with varying unbelievable excuses. This teacher was a middle-aged gentleman who had been patiently teaching Lisa to drive for a good few months. Lisa had good days and off days and was not going to be easily beaten. She was determined that she would pass that test no matter how long it was going to take her.

She had been watching out through her window for Stuart, on the off chance that he would turn up early, already having her coat and driving shoes on when he arrived. Locking her apartment door behind her, she hurried walking down the stairs. Opening the driver's side door she jumped onto the seat, throwing her handbag into the back, the warmth from inside the car hitting her as soon as she opened the door.

"Hi Stuart." Feeling a little nervous because of the recent snowfall Lisa started adjusting her mirrors and the seat.

"Afternoon Lisa and how are you today? There's no need to look so worried, it's only a bit of snow." Stuart looked up at the sky, trying to predict the weather. "Don't think we're going to get any more just yet."

"I'm feeling determined. This is going to be a good lesson," Lisa said, trying to convince herself whilst turning her head to smile at him. "How are you today?"

"I'm not too bad thank you. I can't complain, well I would but I don't think anyone would want to listen." Stuart was always a polite man, who she had never witnessed grumbling about anybody or anything. "I've had the car repaired so if we can avoid bumping into things today then that would be great."

Lisa smiled whilst shrugging her shoulders. "Sorry again."

Stuart returned the smile. He was a frail looking greying man who always looked like he could do with a good scrub and often smelt of stale whisky. Lisa liked him though; he always remained calm under any given situation.

"When you're ready Lisa, I'd like you to pull out and drive down the road." Stuart looked relaxed whilst making himself comfortable. "Take it nice and slowly, it will be slippery in places."

Checking her mirrors and looking over her shoulder Lisa indicated to pull out. Stuart put his arm around the back of Lisa's headrest and double checked, looking over his right shoulder. "That's good." Stuart said, nodding his head in approval. "If you can drive on a bit further and then take the second turn on your left by the old telephone box. We'll drive to one of the side roads up there and practice a bit of reversing around the corner."

Lisa had her determined head on and listened very carefully, following his every instruction. Passing her theory test a few months before was the easy part for her, manoeuvring forward was satisfactory; reversing was a totally different story.

"That's much better, Lisa. You must be feeling a whole lot more confident now." Stuart's phone beeped, he checked the message before continuing. "We'll just have another go at that and then we'll have a quick refresher on a three-point turn. I know that you are capable, I just want to give you some more practice."

Handling the car well on both the reversing and the three-point turn Lisa returned to the main road and drove on further to another side road. "Now I know that you haven't done this before but I'm going to show you how to parallel park." Stuart looked more confident than how Lisa had felt.

Her eyes widened. "Erm right, I'm not too sure about that. I don't think I'm quite ready for that yet."

Stuart continued with the encouragement. "You'll be fine, just start turning that wheel when I tell you to. Trust me."

Her hour's lesson was soon over, Stuart asked her to drive back to her apartment. "Not bad today Lisa. We just need to have a few more lessons like this and then you will be ready to go in for your test." Stuart said with sincerity. "Same time next week then?"

Feeling an air of excitement alongside of her achievement, she reached onto the back seat and grabbed her bag. "Yes please Stuart and thank you so much for being so patient with me."

Stuart had leaned over Lisa to turn off the engine. "You've done really well today. You need to start believing in yourself a bit more. I have had far worse drivers than you and managed to get them through their tests. Next lesson

I want to see a much more positive attitude because I know that you will do just fine."

Climbing out, she bent down and looked into the car. "Bye Stuart, I'll see you next week."

Feeling proud of herself she left the car door open for Stuart to get into the driver's side. Half way along the path she turned around and gave Stuart a little wave before walking back up to her apartment, part of her wanting to do a hop, skip and a jump. A well-earned drinking chocolate was in order, with fresh cream and marshmallows.

It had been a few years since Lisa had moved into her apartment. She had settled in comfortably and felt very much at home. It looked quite different from when she had first moved in, making quite a few alterations and totally redecorating it. The plant life along with the candles had taken over however.

Lisa still enjoyed working at Woodhayes Bed and Breakfast and religiously went walking on Sundays with the same group of people, having her Sunday dinner at The Red Squirrel. She loved the routine, her friends and that feeling of belonging somewhere.

Lisa had not been interested in having a man in her life up until a new member, who had just moved into the area, joined their walking group. Being quite content with her life, she had not really wanted to complicate things by trying to trust again. Feeling somehow magnetised to him, she found him mesmerising but was unsure as to why. He was a good ten years older than Lisa, appearing to be quite shy at first, not making eye contact, let alone speaking to Lisa the first few times he walked with the group. Initially keeping himself to himself, he did not go along to the pub with them after either.

It was not until a few weeks had gone by that Lisa decided to pick up the courage to introduce herself to him. Standing there, by himself, waiting for the others in the group to arrive Lisa saw her opportunity and pounced. "Hi, I'm Lisa. I'm pleased to meet you," Lisa said, holding out her hand to shake his, giving him one of her big smiles.

Taken by surprise, he held out his hand. "Hello Lisa, I'm William but my friends call me Bill."

Feeling presumptuous with a twinkle in her eye Lisa continued. "Hi Bill. I've seen you a few times, how are you enjoying the walking group?"

"Yes, it's good. Well I must be enjoying it; I keep coming back for more, don't I?"

Smiling she turned around when she heard the familiar chatter of her Sunday afternoon companions coming from behind her whilst they walked up the road. Most of the group, who were attending, had arrived.

Lisa turned back around to Bill and tried to get the flow of some type of a conversation going again. "Do you mind if I walk with you?"

Bill had already set off walking, on hearing Lisa's question he responded. "No not at all, it would be nice to have a walking buddy."

Catching him up, she walked alongside him. The walk was quiet, it was not too long before the group had walked up into the hills and had decided to stop to take advantage of the breath-taking scenery. Lisa poured herself a drink of tea from her flask. The steam from the cup was denser than the vapour that was coming from Lisa's breathing.

"Would you like some tea?" Lisa asked Bill before taking a sip herself.

"No, I'm fine thank you." Bill stared out at the views, admiring the astonishing landscape.

"Doesn't the snow make the scenery look even more breath-taking?" Lisa said whilst never tiring and appreciating its beauty too.

"It certainly does," Bill said, not taking his eyes away from the panoramic horizon.

"I could stand up here forever. It's a beautiful sunny day too. You have to make the most of days like today." Lisa chattered away, seemingly oblivious to Bill's need for peace and quiet. "I think it's forecast to be sunny for most of the week. I hope that it doesn't make the snow melt too quickly."

"No, that would be a shame." Bill turned his gaze away from the views and looked at Lisa, realising that they had a shared interest in not only walking but nature also.

Lisa was keen to learn more about him. "How long have you lived around here Bill?"

Appearing self-conscious, his answer was short. "Not very long, just a few months."

Reaching into her rucksack, she got out a pen and wrote down her telephone number in the corner of a magazine. "Just in case you need to get in touch or need advice about anything locally." Tearing it off, she passed it to Bill. "Get in touch anytime."

Reaching out his hand, he smiled; taking the scrap of paper, he put it into his jacket pocket.

The group started with their walk back to the village. Lisa tagged alongside Bill.

"Why don't you come and have your Sunday lunch with the rest of us. I'm always starving by the time we've finished walking. They do a lovely Sunday roast at our local. It's reasonably priced too," Lisa said, unable to contain her enthusiasm. "Unless you've got to be somewhere."

"Sounds tempting. It would be rude for me to say no, wouldn't it?" Bill said, following on behind her to the Red Squirrel.

Bill did not really say very much whilst they were all eating. He was polite and answered questions that he was asked and smiled when someone said something funny. He had only just eaten his meal and had not even finished chewing his food when he stood up to put his jacket on. "My apologies I'm going to have to make tracks now. I've got a few jobs to sort out, that really need to be done before I go back to work tomorrow. I'll see you all next week." Smiling he put up his hand to give a small wave. Each said their goodbyes back to him. "It's been good talking to you Lisa."

Lisa tried not to look disappointed, smiling she waved goodbye to him.

He was in her thoughts a lot that following week. Lisa even kept an eye out for him when she was out and about and made sure that she had sufficient make-up on just in case they should happen to bump into each other.

Bill was not there to join the walking group the following Sunday. Feeling concerned that she may have been too forward and scared him off; she kept her fingers crossed the following week in hope that she would see him again.

Lisa's prayers were answered, he was there. Walking just ahead of her, she hurried to catch him up. "Hi Bill," Lisa said, smiling sweetly at him.

Looking genuinely embarrassed Bill said, "Hi... I'm really sorry; I've forgotten your name."

"It's Lisa!" Her smile soon faded whilst her pace slowed down, allowing Bill to walk ahead alone if he chose to.

Bill slowed down too, turning his head to continue their conversation. "Sorry Lisa. How are you? I'm absolutely useless with names. I hope you can forgive me."

Tucking her hair behind her ears she felt instantly uplifted, forgetting about his lapse of memory. "Yes, don't worry about it. I'm good, how about you?"

"Yes, I'm not too bad thank you. I really needed to get out for this walk today. It certainly is doing me the power of good." Bill appeared to be pushing himself more than usual, his strides were longer and his pace was quicker.

Over the following weeks, Lisa found that Bill had started to come out of his shell more, feeling like they had got much closer, walking and chatting each Sunday.

"Are you going to be joining us for Sunday dinner again today?" He would often make up an excuse and did not always join them.

Feeling the need to rub his stomach whilst responding, he said, "Sounds great because I missed breakfast this morning."

Raising an eyebrow, Lisa cheekily said, "Good, because it's your turn to buy the wine."

It was Lisa's turn to leave early that Sunday, having an earlier start than usual on the Monday. Whilst grabbing her bag and coat Lisa said her goodbyes to everyone. Bill stood up too, putting on his jacket he followed Lisa outside. Before reaching the door, Bill gently put his hand on her shoulder to get her attention. "Would it be okay to go back to yours for a coffee?"

Feeling a little surprised mixed in with an amount of excitement, Lisa said, "Yes of course."

"Lead the way." Bill waited for Lisa to continue walking before following her, unsure as to which direction she would go in.

They talked and laughed and it was not too long before they had got back to Lisa's place. Lisa unlocked the door whilst they tried to catch their breath after the climb up the stairs, which had appeared to be more difficult with both the large intake of food and the already long walk previous to that.

Bill bent down to take off his shoes, hanging his coat up he quickly glanced around the room. "Nice place you have here."

Lisa walked into the kitchen. Putting the kettle on, she proudly said, "Thank you. I like it anyway."

Showing Bill around she explained everything that she had done to the place, going into fine detail about her 'do it yourself' skills, before they sat on the sofa and finished drinking their coffees. Time flew by quickly as they chatted, putting the world to rights.

Looking at his wristwatch, Bill looked disappointed as he said. "I'd better get going Lisa, so you can have that early night you were wanting. Thanks for the coffee."

Taking the cup from his hand, she showed him to the door. After putting his shoes and jacket back on, he leant forward and kissed her tenderly on the cheek. Feeling like a little girl again, she felt herself blush. Holding her face gently underneath her chin he smiled at her. "I'll see you next Sunday Lisa."

"I'll look forward to it." Lisa looked at his lips and could not resist kissing him. Closing her eyes, the kiss was returned.

As the weeks went by Bill started to confide in Lisa more, explaining how he had been hurt on more than one occasion with bad relationships in the past and that is why he wanted to take things slowly. He was a thoughtful lover and would make Lisa feel like she was wanted and very special. She had truly fallen for him and was in love all over again.

A steady flow of flowers would be hand delivered by Bill or by a florist to both her work and home. Never having flowers bought for her even once before she often found it overwhelming. Writing her poetry, he would leave it in strategic places, so that she would find it when he was not there.

Nearly a year had passed by before Lisa had decided to start pushing the commitment subject. Bill was still dragging his feet.

Lisa's eyes looked sad and wanting as she begged Bill to stay over, her head resting on his shoulder whilst her hand stroked through his chest hair. "Please stay over tonight. It would be lovely to see you there when I wake up in the morning."

Without even giving it any thought, he squeezed her shoulder with his hand and kissed her on the forehead. "I'm sorry Lisa; I can't, not yet anyway."

Lisa's frustrations had started to show, a frown appearing on her face. "Why not?"

Bill remained composed as he held her closely to him. "I just don't want to rush things between us. Things are fine the way they are, aren't they?"

Pulling away from him, she looked at him, challenging him further. "Please Bill; it's been a year now. I wouldn't say that's rushing things. I have always been so patient. It's as though you don't really want us to be together, not properly anyway."

Bill tried to calm the situation by stroking her cheek. "Soon Lisa, I promise."

"I love you Bill," Lisa said, trying to make a last ditched effort.

Bill's facial expression turned to one of surprise.

Without giving him time to respond, she snapped. "Oh just go... Get out!"

Bill quietly and calmly collected his belongings together and upon leaving closed the door gently behind him. Lisa remained seated, she did not chase after him and she refused to shed a tear.

Bill did not attend the next Sunday's walking group. Lisa did not see or hear from him, there were no telephone calls, no flowers or poetry. The more Lisa struggled to put him out of her mind the more she actually thought about him, especially when she was laid in her bed at night, all alone, trying to rest but her mind would not allow it.

A few weeks had passed by and Lisa had just started to cope with the situation when without warning there was a knock on her door. Bill stood there in the doorway looking apologetic with a single red rose in his hand. "I've missed you Lisa." He was the last person she expected to see stood there.

Lisa was not sure if to hug him or slam the door in his face. "Have you indeed?" Standing there she waited for his response, her facial expression did not give away how she was feeling inside.

Looking like a schoolboy waiting outside the headmaster's office he said, "Yes, I have."

Standing to one side, she indicated for him to enter by waving him in. Closing the door behind him, she stood leaning with her back to the door. Their serious facial expressions remained. Scowling at him, the scolding commenced. "You hurt me Bill and I deserve better than that. You disappeared and I've not heard anything from you. Where the hell have you been? You only needed to say if you needed some space."

Bowing his head in shame, he had no rational explanation to give. Reaching out Lisa took the rose from his hand and started to help him take off his jacket. An earnest expression replaced with a smile as he leant forward to take off his shoes.

Lisa had missed him terribly, holding out her hand she succumbed, leading him into the bedroom. Putting the rose down at the foot of the bed they sat for a while on the edge, in a comfortable silence, holding hands. Bill looked at Lisa, a passion burning in his eyes. He waited patiently for her to make the first move. Unable to resist him, it was not long until they made love. Laying together in each other's arms, their exhausted, over-heating perspiring bodies close, the comfortable silence continued.

Bill broke the silence. "I've missed you so much these last two weeks. I've not been able to get you out of my mind." He kissed her passionately, his hands holding her face. "I want you to know that I love you too Lisa. My life is just complicated."

It was her turn to remain silent as she held him close to her. She could feel his slow, strong heartbeat pulsating whilst her own heart was full of love, she was so grateful that he had come back to her. Concluding to do things at his pace, she had decided not to put any more pressure on him.

"I would like to stay with you tonight." Bill kissed her again, this time gently on her forehead, before continuing. "If you'd still like me to?"

Nodding her head, she looked up at him, smiling.

They talked for hours; Lisa kept him up-to-date with the local gossip, her main reliable source being the Bed and Breakfast. Allowing Lisa to do most of the talking he explained that he had been busy with his work.

The darkness seemed to arrive quickly, the time had flown by. They had long since stopped talking, Lisa felt drowsy but was not quite asleep. So as not to waken her Bill slowly slipped out of bed. Picking up his trousers from the bedroom floor, he reached into the pocket for his phone, taking it to the bathroom with him, unaware that Lisa had not quite drifted off to sleep. Intrigued she laid still and listened carefully, curious as to who he was going to ring.

Hearing him clearly, his whisper was not quiet and the sound travelled. Slurring his words as though drunk, he began his explanation. "Listen darling, I'm not going to make it back home tonight, I've had one too many and definitely can't drive back. I'm going to crash at Gavin's... Yes I know darling and I'm really sorry... I'll get back as soon as I can in the morning... Will do... Yes... Take care... I love you too."

Disbelief came over Lisa, her head started to spin and she could not think straight with all sorts of ideas going around inside her head. Was he married? Did he already have a girlfriend or was it just a family member?

Bill turned off the bathroom light and crept back into bed. Feeling sick to the stomach Lisa laid still with her eyes shut and remained calm. Her heart pounded against her ribcage, the thumping pulsating in her ears. Bill laid beside Lisa, stroking her face he whispered in her ear, "I love you Lisa."

Lisa wanted it to be so true. Moving away from Bill she squirmed, sitting upright she started to get out of bed, sliding her feet into her slippers. Walking towards the door she reached up to a hook to retrieve her dressing gown. Putting it on, she walked out of the bedroom.

Bill sat up, the realisation hitting him, the evidence on his face. "Lisa, is everything okay?"

She remained calm, not wanting to get angry she had wanted to walk away from the situation and calm down first. "I'm suddenly not tired any more. I need a drink."

Bill followed her into the kitchen with an aura of guilt and horror combined. Lisa was sitting in her usual chair with her back to him.

"Did you hear me in the bathroom?" Bill asked, first checking before needing to explain himself. "We need to talk. I need to explain. It's not what it seems."

Lisa had been down this road before and did not want history to repeat itself. Remaining seated with her back to him, she was unable to face him. "You don't need to explain anything to me. It is what it is. You just need to get your things and go."

"I am so, so sorry Lisa. I should have told you when we first met. You and I were never supposed to happen. I thought we would just be friends." Bill's eyes filled with tears. "I'm married. My wife is wheelchair bound, not that that is a good excuse. She's in that chair because she was in a car crash, a crash that I was in too and a crash that I caused. I had been drink driving."

Lisa turned her head around to look at him, her mouth gaped open. "Oh my God. That's so awful." Standing up she leant on the back of another chair and listened intently to him.

"I was young and foolish. She was my girlfriend at the time. We'd had an argument in the pub one night. She stormed out and I went after her in my car. She didn't want to get in because I'd been drinking." The tears were flowing down his cheeks. "I jumped out of the car and tried to drag her into the car. Gillian eventually got in but we carried on arguing. I got more and more angry and drove faster, losing control I hit a tree. The rest is history."

Pausing, he was obviously choked and still racked with guilt. Calming himself down, he continued. "I can't even remember what we were arguing about, it was something petty. I got out of the car without even a scratch. Gillian was seriously hurt and it was all my fault. I spent every waking hour with her until she came out of hospital. I proposed to her while she laid there in her hospital bed and gave her my word that I would look after her forever. I owed her that much." Bill's eyes were now red and his face was blotchy as he looked at Lisa for help with an expression of bewilderment.

It was Lisa's turn to have her say. "Oh my God, Bill. You should have told me earlier. We could just have been friends before allowing things to go so far. If I had known I wouldn't have come on so heavy with you. It all makes sense now. Why you wanted to take things so slowly, why I went for periods of time without seeing you, why I've never even met any of your friends or family and why I wasn't allowed to contact you. I feel such a fool, the signs were staring me right in the face."

Bill wiped his tears away from his face with the back of his hand. "Don't you see, Lisa?" He looked relieved that the truth was now out in the open.

Lisa shook her head, shrugging her shoulder she said. "See what?"

"I love you," Bill said. "I can't help the way I feel and I want to be with you."

Taking a deep breath, her heart and head in total conflict. "Don't you see Bill?" Lisa smiled, a smile that revealed her remorse. "We can't be together, no matter how much we love each other. It's not fair to Gillian and it's not fair to me. I don't want to be your mistress, your bit on the side and you can't break your promise to your wife either, she needs you."

"It's so not fair. I made a stupid mistake when I was young and now I have to pay for it for the rest of my life. I don't even love my wife, I don't think I've ever really loved her. I just feel pity for her," Bill said. "It's eating away at me from the inside."

Frowning, she couldn't believe the words that she was hearing. "Imagine how your wife feels. It's not fair to her either. I won't allow you to leave her for me. I just wish you had told me a lot sooner and then it wouldn't have come to this. I would just have left you alone, no matter how strong my feelings."

Getting down on his knees in front of her, he pleaded with her. "Please Lisa, we can work something out. We have to work it out."

"I'm going to go back to bed now knowing that your friendship is still very important to me. You can stay tonight if you want but you must leave in the morning and go back to your wife." Lisa was adamant and would not be changing her mind.

No more words were spoken; the sadness on both their faces said it all. Lisa took off her dressing gown and slippers and got back into bed. Bill climbed into bed at the side of her, putting his arms around her, he held her close.

The streetlight outside gave little light through Lisa's curtains into her bedroom. Catching sight of a number of small black shadows swaying gently about on her bedroom floor, she drifted off to sleep, too exhausted to care.

The ticking of the clock and the rain tapping against the window were the only sounds that broke the silence, as Lisa floated above her bed just underneath the ceiling. She had only floated a handful of times in her life and was not sure how or why she did it. It was a controlled floating feeling, the same sensation you get when you are on water. An enormous house spider was crawling creepily along the top of the duvet, Lisa watched it to make sure that it did not go anywhere near her face. Crawling down the side it appeared to take refuge underneath her bed.

Bill was no longer cuddled up to Lisa, they both slept soundly looking peacefully right together.

In that same moment the bedroom door opened slightly. Lisa turned her head and witnessed the small black shadows that she had seen earlier drifting out through the gap. Returning her attention to Bill she watched him sleeping. The bedroom door opened wider, the large black shadow appeared and entered. It had not noticed Lisa levitating above. Hovering towards the bed it looked over Lisa's body, leaning forward until its face was close to hers. Intrigued Lisa watched it closely. Straightening back up it moved around to Bill's side of the bed before leaning forward until it was close to his face before slowly turning its head upwards to look at where Lisa was hovering. Lisa unsure, slowly tipped her head to one side. The black shadow copied her. Not wanting it to hurt Bill she shook her head slowly. The black shadow straightened up and moved backwards away from Bill and slowly faded away.

The sound of the alarm clock woke Lisa the following morning. Turning it off within seconds, the noise being too loud for her first thing. Bill slept on, not stirring. After Lisa had her morning stretch she shuffled her feet along the floor in the direction of the kitchen, finding it particularly hard to wake up that morning. The light from the fridge was bright as she looked for the orange juice with just one squinted eye open.

Bill had started to stir from his deep sleep. Turning over he noticed that Lisa had already got up and soon followed her into the kitchen.

Entering the kitchen, he greeted Lisa. "Morning Lisa. How are you this morning? Did you sleep well?"

Lisa, unsure as to why it was called beauty sleep, felt more like a troll whilst turning round to look at Bill. "Morning. On and off. Will you do me a massive favour before you go?"

"Yes," Bill said without a second thought. "Anything."

Grimacing, Lisa said, "I think I saw a massive spider under the bed last night. Will you have a look for me?"

Bill went back into the bedroom, getting down onto his hands and knees he lifted up the duvet to look underneath the bed. "I can't see anything." Looking again, he gasped. "Oh wait, I think it's up there, living in the corner."

Lisa had already plugged the vacuum cleaner in ready and was handing Bill the nozzle. "Wow, he's a big one. Can't we just put him outside?"

Flicking the socket switch, the vacuum cleaner went into action. "No, just kill it," Lisa said, over the noise of the vac. "I don't want that damn thing coming back in."

Manoeuvring himself into a better position Bill laid on his back on the floor, he was ready for action. The spider had heard the commotion and tried to make a run for it, the nozzle was only just big enough to suck it up.

Flicking the switch off, she breathed out a sigh of relief. "Thank you. I absolutely hate spiders. Can I make you some breakfast as a reward?"

"No thanks." Bill smiled picking up his clothes from the bedroom floor. "I'd better be going. I don't want to prolong this agony any longer."

Her heart sunk, she knew deep down that it was for the best. Reaching out she stroked his cheek. "Okay."

Bill's eyes looked sad. "Unless you've changed your mind."

"No Bill I haven't changed my mind and I won't be doing either." Lisa paused. "Look after Gillian."

Getting dressed he was ready to go. "I still love you Lisa."

The once comfortable atmosphere was replaced with awkwardness. "I know. We can still be friends though, right?"

He smiled. "I'd love a hug before I go," Bill said.

Hugging each other tight, they both knew it was definitely over. There would be no going back.

"Now go," Lisa said, "Before I start crying."

Lisa watched as Bill put his shoes and coat on. Looking back at her, he gave her a little wave. "Goodbye Lisa. Take care of yourself."

Giving him a half-hearted smile, she gave him a little wave before he closed the door behind him. "Goodbye Bill," Lisa said to herself. "I love you too."

Giving out a big sigh she really was not in the mood for going to work, she had to set off in half an hour. Finishing her juice, she put the glass down in the sink and went to the bathroom to turn on the shower. Whilst the shower was running and warming up Lisa brushed her teeth over the washbasin, the bathroom mirror had become steamed up. Reaching up she wiped the mirror with the flat of her hand, not clearing it totally, she noticed that the black shadow was in the bathroom with her, it was standing right behind her. Turning around quickly to look, it had gone. Wiping the mirror again with a facecloth she stared at her own reflection, there was no black shadow behind her but instead a face of someone she barely recognised. Her face was pale, cheeks sunken in, dark around the eyes; her eyes seemed to be bigger and stood out more. She could not look any more; her own reflection's stare scared her, made the hairs on the back of her neck stand up. Her eyes were pure evil.

Getting undressed she stood under the warm water of the shower, allowing it to pour through her hair, over her face and down over her body. For the first time since she had moved into the apartment, she felt empty and all alone again.

Chapter Eight

Home Sweet Home

Pulling up outside the driving test centre Lisa felt quietly confident and less nervous than she had initially anticipated. Two other learner cars had pulled up at the same time, both drivers looked younger, one of them did not even look old enough to be behind the wheel of a car. Her test was one of the first on that day and it was the school holidays, so the roads were reasonably quiet without parents on the school run. The examiner was an older lady who was really nice to her, being nowhere near as scary as the horror stories she had heard about from other people's experiences. Pretending that Stuart was sitting in the back of the car made the test feel more comfortable, imagining his voice guiding her patiently when receiving instructions from the examiner. Throughout the test, her head movements were exaggerated when she checked her mirrors and even managed not to bounce off any kerbs or any other stationary objects.

The examiner carefully put her flowery patterned clipboard down onto her lap and looked over her spectacles at Lisa. "Congratulations, I'm pleased to tell you that you have passed your practical driving test." Putting out her hand, she shook Lisa's hand.

Lisa felt that the test had gone well but for a brief moment, she expected the examiner to tell her that she had failed because of the serious expression that was on her face. "Wow, I can't quite believe it." Now on cloud nine she gave out a little screech of excitement. "Thank you so much."

The examiner filled out the necessary paperwork before handing it to Lisa, giving her a warm friendly smile. "Excellent driving, only a couple of minors. I hope you enjoy the rest of your day."

Stuart had been waiting for Lisa outside the test centre. Sitting patiently on an old wooden bench, he stood up when he saw Lisa park perfectly on the road nearby. Jumping out of the car, she ran straight over to him. The examiner followed close behind, handing the car keys over to Stuart. Before Lisa had even spoken, he had worked out the outcome of her test from her obvious uncontained excitement.

Raising her eyebrows Lisa grinned from ear to ear. "I've passed." Grabbing Stuart, she gave him a big squeeze and a gentle peck on his cheek. "I just can't believe it."

Taken by surprise, Stuart had never received such overwhelming gratitude. "Fantastic Lisa. I told you that you could do it. I'll drive you back to your apartment because I think you need to calm down before getting back behind the wheel."

"Thanks Stuart. I really could not have done it without you." Lisa walked back over to the car and waited patiently for Stuart, who had gone off for a chat with the examiner. Leaning against the car she tried to lip-read, to no avail, they were quite a distance away and it was not really one of her skills.

After shaking the examiner's hand Stuart strolled back towards the car. The drive back to the apartment was one filled with lots of chatting and laughter.

Lisa had already booked a day's holiday from work, what followed her test could have had two possible outcomes. If she had failed, she was going to spend the rest of the day wallowing in self-pity, eating chocolate and watching rubbish on daytime television. That certainly was not going to happen, instead she would test drive a few cars that she had already taken a shine to and had been researching for months.

After a couple of hours of getting in and out of cars Lisa decided that before making a final decision on which car to purchase she would go into the Red Squirrel for a late lunch. Not usually going during the week, she decided that she deserved a treat.

The barman who was a young man that looked fresh out of college and of casual appearance lacked any type of enthusiasm. "What can I get for you?"

Not tempted by her usual large glass of red wine, she fancied something nutritional instead and would, hopefully, be purchasing a car later on that afternoon, so alcohol would not be a good idea. "I'll have an orange juice please."

The barman picked harshly at a very noticeable spot on his chin. "Can I order you any food to go with that?"

If she had not been so hungry that could possibly have put her off. "Yes, I fancy a cheese and ham toasty with a side order of chips please." It was the first thing that came to mind and her body appeared to have a craving.

"Any garlic bread to go with that?" Lisa wondered how many times he had said that since his shift had started, due to the fact that he sounded like he was reading from a script and would have preferred to be anywhere but there.

Lisa forced a smile before answering. "No thank you."

Tearing off the sheet from his little order pad, he passed it to a female colleague, who looked just as enthusiastic and was sitting on a stool behind the bar. How Lisa had not noticed her straight away was anybody's guess, she was covered in tattoos and body piercings, not the usual look for the Red Squirrel.

Pouring the orange juice into a glass, he placed it down onto the bar. "That will be six pounds and seventy five pence and I'll give you a shout when your food is ready."

Handing over a ten-pound note, she gave the barman another exaggerated smile.

Smiling back at her, he said. "Three pounds and twenty-five pence change." He continued with his smile until Lisa had stopped looking at him, be it sarcastic or not she was happy that she had managed to change his mood.

Putting her change away in her purse, she zipped it up, picked up her drink and turned around to look for somewhere to sit. Directly behind her was Bill and his wife sat with him, in her wheelchair with her back to her. Bill looked up, saw Lisa and smiled. She had not seen him for weeks, feeling butterflies in her stomach she smiled back. He looked well and he looked happy. Lisa had to make an instant decision, should she go over and say hello or ignore him and go and sit somewhere else.

Not giving the idea of ignoring him a second thought and as if by magic or some type of animal magnetism she walked over and stood at the side of Gillian's wheelchair, so that she was able to see her. Smiling firstly at Gillian, she was more interested in concentrating her efforts on Bill.Stopping the urge to hug and kiss him Lisa's eyes had clearly lit up. "Hi Bill, how are you? I haven't seen you for ages. I hope you're keeping well." Not giving him chance to answer the words poured from her mouth.

Remaining composed Bill looked straight over at Gillian. "Hi, Lisa. Gillian, this is Lisa."

Feeling awkward, Lisa was hesitant if she should try to shake her hand, unsure if she was even able to move it. "Hi Gillian."

Fortunately, Gillian lifted her hand and held it out for Lisa. "Hi Lisa." Moving she turned to look at Bill trustfully, "How do you two know each other?"

Bill was quick off the mark, wanting to answer before Lisa got in there first. "From that walking group I used to go to."

"Oh, that's nice," Gillian said, totally oblivious to her husband's once infidelity.

An awkward silence followed whilst Lisa realised how much she had missed him, if only as a friend.

Quickly thinking of something to break the silence, Lisa said. "I've not seen you there for a while. Are you not going to be going anymore?"

"I've just been too busy, what with work and looking after Gillian," Bill said, with a stereotypical answer whilst staring at the table.

Gillian interrupted melodramatically. "That and there was a woman at the group that got on his nerves and had started to become a bit of a nuisance."

A lump appeared in Lisa's throat. Following a loud gulp, she said, "Oh." Not wanting to give away how hurt she felt by that comment she managed to hold back her tears. "I'm sorry to hear about that. I think I know who you mean."

Lisa looked down at Gillian; she was far more attractive than what she had pictured in her mind and was not at all dependent on Bill, appearing to be perfectly capable of looking after herself. Having beautiful long black curly hair and big blue eyes, she kept herself well-groomed in appearance. Lisa looked away before Gillian caught her staring. Appearing slightly nervous, Bill smiled up at Lisa whilst Gillian was not looking. The atmosphere was becoming more awkward by the minute.

The barman interrupted, placing the plate onto the bar, he looked over in Lisa's direction and said, "Your toasty and chips are ready."

"Wow that was quick. Well it was good to see you Bill and lovely to meet you Gillian. I'll leave you both to it and I hope you enjoy the rest of your day." Lisa felt relieved of the excuse to walk away.

"Yes good to see you too, Lisa," Bill said, as an afterthought as she walked to the furthest possible table from them. Putting down her drink, she walked back over to the bar and collected her food.

"Knives and forks are just over there," The barman said, pointing his finger in the direction of the cutlery trolley.

"Thanks," Lisa said, even though she knew her way around the pub with her eyes shut.

Overhearing Gillian and Bill talk as she walked back past them, she pretended that she had not heard them and that she was in a world of her own.

"Lisa seems really pleasant." Gillian said, looking directly at Bill.

"She's okay," Bill said, in a matter of fact way before taking another mouthful of his beer. Feeling paranoid, part of him wondered if Gillian was actually wanting some kind of reaction from him, if she already knew everything and was in fact testing the water.

Picking up the vinegar bottle from the table she doused her chips with it before starting to nibble on them. Her feelings for Bill were still the same; she still loved him and hoped that in time those feelings would go. Needing to keep herself busy and focused with more important matters at hand, Lisa started to think about the cars she had just taken for a test drive. In reality, her mind had already been made up before she had actually walked into the pub, just giving herself a little bit more time to make sure that she did not change her mind.

Lisa saw Bill standing up; he was making his way to the gent's toilet. Looking away, she tried her best not to look at him. Succeeding when he went in, she accidentally forgot to make the effort, looking up when he came back out. He smiled over at her. If he was expecting a smile back then he would be sadly disappointed. She looked straight through him, like he was not even there.

Bill had the smile wiped from his face; putting on his jacket, he wheeled Gillian out of the pub.

Feeling both saddened and slightly relieved at the same time Lisa continued to eat her lunch and finished off her drink. Feeling bloated and uncomfortable after eating her food too quickly she stood up to put on her jacket, picking up her handbag she put the strap over her shoulder. Collecting her glass and plate, she walked over to the bar and placed them on the top.

"Thank you," Lisa said, smiling at both of the bar staff in turn. They both looked weary and were now the only two people left in the pub.

"You're welcome," The barman said whilst looking at his wristwatch.

Repeatedly looking down out of her apartment window Lisa could not believe that she had purchased her first car, a black Volkswagen Golf.

Still full from her lunch she could only manage a little bit of fruit for her dinner before running herself a nice warm bubble bath. Turning on the hot water tap in the bathroom, her landline telephone started to ring in the other room. It was loud and persistent and very difficult to ignore. Picking it up, she was not quite sure who to expect on the other end. "Hello."

"Hi Lisa." It was Bill, his voice was friendly and his memory was obviously short. "How are you?"

A short pause followed whilst she composed herself, finding it hard to believe his cheek. Part of her wanted to tell him where to go but decided it was always best to be polite. "I'm fine, thank you Bill. What can I do for you?" Her once friendly tone had been replaced with a more professional manner.

The desperation in his voice was evident. "I need to see you."

Finding it hard to remain polite, her voice now sounded abrupt. "You saw me earlier. Why do you need to see me again?"

His desperation could now be mistaken for sounding pathetic. "To say how sorry I am and to tell you how much I miss you."

"Apology accepted. Now we both need to move on." Lisa surprised herself on how strong she was being. "I've got to go, I'm running myself a bath and I don't want it to overflow."

Bill must have known that his persistence would not work, not this time. "Please, I need to see you."

"I really don't think that's a good idea. Do you?" She so wanted to see him too but was not giving anything away with the way that she sounded and acted.

"I really am so very sorry. I need to explain to your face Lisa." He had started to sniffle, as though he was crying.

"There's really no need. Take care of yourself Bill and take care of that lovely wife of yours." Lisa put the receiver down gently before Bill had chance to say anything else. Sighing deeply, she had now mastered the art of holding back her tears.

Reaching for her hairbrush from the bed, she started to tie up her hair as she walked back towards the bathroom, the telephone started to ring again. Ignoring it at first, she carried on in a daze and watched the bubbles rising in the bath water. It rang off and started to ring again. Turning off the hot water tap, Lisa surrendered and went to answer it again, deciding that she would answer it one last time and then leave it off the hook.

It was Susan on the other end and she sounded panicked. "Is that you Lisa?"

Surprised to hear from her sister, she had not seen or heard from her for a good long while. "Susan, is that you? Whatever is the matter?"

With a degree of bossiness to her manner, Susan said, "Lisa, I've been trying to ring you, your phone has either been engaged or just ringing out. Its Mum, she's had a bad fall down the stairs."

"Is she going to be okay?" Usually Lisa was the last to know or totally left out of the loop when it had anything to do with family business.

"She keeps asking for you Lisa. She wants to see you, as soon as you can."

"Okay. I'll grab some things and I'll be there as soon as." Although the timing was not right, Lisa had been bursting to tell someone her news all day. "Susan, I'm so excited. I passed my driving test today and bought my first car."

Susan tried to sound happy for her but she appeared more anxious than anything else. "Wow, well done you, congratulations and I'll see you soon."

"Yes, I'll meet you at Mum and Dad's house." Tilting her head to one side, she moved the handset of the telephone away from her ear and looked at it. Susan had already put down the receiver before Lisa had finished, which left her feeling unsure if she had caught the rendezvous.

Knowing that she would have to go back there one day and it had been some time since she had seen the rest of the family she started to pack a bag for a few days, unsure as to how long she would be there for.

On her way, she drove down to Woodhayes Bed and Breakfast to update them on what had been happening, first giving them the good news before the bad. They were understanding, as usual, and Lisa had plenty of holiday left to take anyway.

Lisa had no motorway driving experience, only what she had read from books and watched on the internet. Not expecting to be on the motorway quite so quickly, she had hoped to have a few lessons with Stuart first. Staying mainly in the left hand lane, she tried to relax but her shoulders were as stiff as a board. The motorway seemed to go on forever but at least the drive was problem free with no traffic jams and it was not long before Lisa was back on the normal roads again. When closer to her old family home she started to glance out through the side windows, noting that nothing had really changed much, even recognising the same old faces after all that time she had been away.

Driving past Beechwood Park, the journey was almost over. Lisa parked her car just further up the road from her mum and dad's house. Climbing out of her car, she locked it leaving her case in the boot.

It felt strange being back, taking her time whilst absorbing her surroundings. Everything seemed smaller than she remembered it. Knocking on the front door, she went in before anyone had chance to answer it and was greeted by Susan who reached out to Lisa and gave her a big hug.

Susan looked overwhelmed to see her, surprised almost, like she had not expected Lisa to turn up. "It's good to see you Lisa. You look really well."

"It's good to see you too. It's been too long. Is Karl not with you?" Lisa said, looking around to see if anyone else was there with them.

"No. He's busy with his work," Susan said, looking coy.

"Where's Dad?" Lisa said, talking through clenched teeth. "Is he at the hospital with Mum?"

Susan pointed towards the kitchen door. "No, he's in the kitchen opening up a tin of baked beans for his supper. He said he's going to eat them straight out of the can because he can't be bothered to warm them up and because the wife isn't about to clean up after him." Her eyes rolled upwards as she gave a disgusted facial expression.

Finding it hard, Lisa pretended that she actually cared. "How is he though? Is he coping?"

"No idea. You tell me. He's still the same as he always was. A loveable rogue," Susan said, a smile breaking onto her face. Both now smiling at each other they began to laugh.

John walked into the living room; he had not changed much over the years, just older and grumpier with a bit more excess weight around his middle. The house had not changed either; it was in even more need of a lick of paint than ever before. Feeling like time had stood still, even the pictures on the wall were exactly the same and were in precisely the same place.

Walking straight past John, Lisa walked into the kitchen, looking around she noticed that he had not bothered to do any washing up or had even managed to put any of his rubbish into the bin. She started to clear it up from the work surfaces and opened the bin lid, it was already full. Remembering where Elizabeth kept the bin liners she opened the drawer to get one out. Whilst taking the bin lid off the security light in the back garden came on, illuminating the entire garden. It always used to come on and scare the life out of the local cat population. Pulling the liner out of the bin, Lisa started to tie a knot in the top. Her attention was drawn to John's lawn, still in pristine condition. Putting the bag down carefully onto the kitchen floor, she moved closer to the window to try to get a better look. Squinting, she was not mistaken in thinking that there was a black shadow floating about six inches above the lawn. Lisa carried on watching, the shadow slowly turned until it was in an upright position. Turning to face Lisa, it knew she was watching and appeared to sit down.

Lisa started to walk towards the back door, feeling the urge to go outside.

Turning the key in the door she was interrupted by John. He had opened the kitchen door and was standing in the doorway. "How long are you going to be staying? I'm just asking because there's something that I want to watch on the telly," John said harshly, whilst tapping his fingers against the doorframe.

Lisa looked back through the kitchen window before answering; the security light had gone off. The black shadow was no longer visible.

Unsure if the shadow was still there or not she turned back around and tried to start a conversation with John. "Anyway how are you Dad? It's been a while and how's Mum? Have you been up to the hospital to visit her yet?" Lisa looked straight at him whilst waiting for a rude response.

He did not respond, instead he stood and looked vacantly at her. Lisa looked towards Susan, who was standing behind him. Susan rolled her eyes upwards again, shaking her head.

Lisa had long since hardened to John's lack of paternal emotions. "Don't you worry, I won't be staying. I will book myself into that bed and breakfast down the road. I'm only here to see Mum anyway."

John walked back into the living room, without a word or a care in the world and flopped back down into his chair. Having obviously found the time to find replacement batteries he aimed his remote at the television and on it went. It was even the same television set that they had watched when they were little. How it had not worn out was a miracle in itself.

Not giving John any more of their time Lisa and Susan walked out of the front door, shutting it carefully behind them.

Walking down the front garden path Lisa turned to Susan smiling and said, "I'll go and book myself into that 'Valley View Bed and Breakfast' just down the road. Hopefully they will have a room available for me. I don't really think I'd be welcome or it would be a barrel of laughs kipping on Dad's sofa, do you?"

Picking up her pace, Susan looked serious as she followed Lisa down to the car. The years certainly had not been as kind to her, she had not aged well and looked stressed with worry lines across her forehead. "I'll come with you and then we can get straight off up to the hospital. It really is good to see you. You seem different somehow."

Jumping into the driver's seat, Lisa put on her seat belt, looking over at Susan she thought how strange it felt to have her sat at the side of her. Putting the key into the ignition, she turned to look at Susan. "How did she fall?"

Shaking her head, Susan shrugged her shoulders. "I don't know. I know as much as you. We'll have to ask her when we get to the hospital."

Alarm bells had already started to ring in Lisa's head. "Do you really think she will tell us the truth this time? She's protected that man for long enough now."

Turning the ignition, Lisa drove towards Valley View. The rest of the journey was quiet, both were wrapped up in their own thoughts. Booking herself in, she had managed to get the last single room that was left and although not as comfortable as home, it was clean and cosy enough for a few days. Getting her bags from the boot, she carried them up to her room, whilst Susan stayed in the car.

Climbing back into the car, Lisa had still got a spring in her step. "Right let's get up to that hospital. I'll unpack later when I get back."

A short uncomfortable silence at the beginning of the journey was soon interrupted when Susan snapped out of her trance, looking at Lisa she asked. "How's Bill?"

"Yes, Bill's good and so is his wife." Taking her eyes off the road for a short while, Lisa looked over at Susan to look at the reaction on her face.

"What? He's married? Oh my God." Susan's mouth was left agape.

Finding it entertaining, Lisa decided to give her a little bit more of her gossip. "Yes, Gillian seems really nice."

Whatever it was that Susan had been thinking about previously had now been totally eclipsed. "What, you've met her?"

Slowly applying the brakes, Lisa stopped at a red traffic light at a crossing. Nobody was waiting there to cross but a young boy who had obviously pressed the button could be seen running away along the path in the opposite direction. Looking behind him, he would randomly stick out his tongue and put up two fingers.

Sniggering, Lisa did not keep Susan waiting too long before answering, "Indeed, only by accident though. They were sat together in my local pub today."

Susan was without any doubt sickened by what she was hearing. "So you found out that he's married today?"

"No I found that out a while ago. It was the first time I'd seen his wife at all and him for a good long while today." Taking a deep breath Lisa sighed and felt a pang of sadness, no longer feeling like it was something that she wanted to talk about. Realising she wanted to cry, she stopped herself by pretending that she was over him. "It was difficult, but I got through it."

Susan appeared genuinely concerned but still the questions continued. "You must have been mortified. How did you find out?"

Wishing she had not said anything, she knew that until she had finished answering Susan's questions, there would be no end to it. "He was at mine and I heard him on the phone with her. The funny thing is that was the one and only night that he stayed all night at mine. When I asked him he told me everything though." Convincing herself that this made it seem more acceptable.

Pulling away slowly as the traffic light turned to green she found it difficult to concentrate when her mind kept wandering back to think about Bill. Picturing how happy Bill and Gillian were whilst sat together in the pub confirmed that she had made the right decision.

Noticing the button pusher walking just further up the road, Lisa gave him a couple of beeps of her car horn. When he turned around Lisa stuck out her tongue, instead of sticking two fingers up she gave him a little wave.

"Didn't you kick off? You'd been seeing him for months."

Briefly looking sideways at Susan, she gave her answer. "I told him we should just be friends instead. I do understand why he lied to me you know."

Looking smug, Susan wriggled herself backwards into her seat. "You always were the calmer one of us. I would have kicked his arse into his next life."

The questioning had finally come to an end but not before Susan had ended it with an unexplained chortle.

Reaching the ring road Lisa was finally able to concentrate on her driving more. The hospital was just a short distance away. Not yet feeling confident enough and rather than parking in the hospital's main car park Lisa chose one of the side roads instead.

Lisa reached over Susan, getting her purse out of the glove compartment. Locking the car behind them, they walked the rest of the way, following the signs that led them towards the main reception area. It felt a lot colder than earlier making Lisa wish that she had put on a thicker jumper.

A friendly looking young man greeted them from behind his computer. He had obviously been in the warmth for some time, his cheeks were rosy from the warmth.

Lisa remained quiet, allowing Susan to do the talking. "Could you tell us which ward Elizabeth Parkins is on please?"

Looking at his computer screen, he pressed a few keys on his keyboard. "Yes Mrs Parkins is on ward A3, the burns ward."

Frowning, Susan looked at Lisa before turning back to the young man. Taking a deep breath, she looked at him through squinted eyes. "The burns ward? Are you sure? Do you have the right Elizabeth Parkins?"

Looking at his computer screen again, he pressed more buttons on his keyboard before replying. "Yes, there has only been one Elizabeth Parkins admitted."

Not wanting to interrupt, Lisa looked down at her shoes whilst waiting for Susan to make a decision on what they should do next.

Susan had gone a little flushed, it could have either been down to the fact that the hospital was too warm or she had just totally embarrassed herself. "Okay. Thank you." Obvious to everyone what her chosen profession was, her patronising self shining through.

Waiting for a moment, unsure what to do next, Susan turned around and pointed up at the signage hanging from the ceiling that gave the directions to ward A3.

Following Susan and the signs Lisa walked past the gift shop, quickly glancing at bunches of flowers that were for sale. Not having time to stop because Susan was on a mission Lisa would call back there later.

"I don't understand," Susan said, as though a penny had finally dropped. "How did she manage to burn herself falling down the stairs?"

Lisa made no attempt to respond to Susan's question, she did not know the answer. Turning around, Susan looked at Lisa with an expression of confusion, waiting for her to respond.

"The ward direction sign is just down there to the right," Lisa said, pointing at it, trying to change the subject.

A few corridors later and after a trip in a lift, they were finally greeted by a nurse when they entered the ward, a friendly young woman with a strong Eastern European accent. "Ladies, could I ask you both to use the hand sanitizer before you enter?" The nurse pointed behind them towards the unit on the wall, next to the swinging doors entrance.

Neither of them had even noticed the sign when entering, strangely having other things on their minds. Doing as they were asked, they walked back, pushing the button on the unit, it squirted gel into their palms.

Rubbing their hands together, they walked back towards the nurse. Stepping in front of them before interrupting them again. "How can I help you ladies?"

Feeling like she was at school again, part of her waiting to be told off, Lisa said, "We're here to visit our mother, Elizabeth Parkins."

The nurse had obviously had a long shift, her patience now wearing thin. Her mascara had smudged underneath her eyes and she appeared quite flustered, as she tried her best to maintain her professionalism. "You are aware that visiting hours are over. The hours are clearly stated on the door."

Looking at her wristwatch, Lisa had not realised what the time was. It was getting late. Her day off work had turned out to be way more eventful than she had planned. Looking back at the nurse, she spoke gently, hoping that she had not had a wasted journey. "No, I'm sorry we didn't realise. I've travelled a long way especially to visit my mum though. Could we not just pop in to say a quick hello? We won't cause any disruption."

"Okay but only for a short while and in future if you could stick to the visiting hours please." The nurse hurriedly escorted them to where Elizabeth was. "Please follow me. I will show you to her bed."

The ward was quiet, some of the patients had already gone to sleep. Others were either sat up reading or watching their own televisions with headphones on.

Reaching a side ward with four beds in, Elizabeth was in the corner near to the window. The nurse pointed to her.

"Thank you," Susan said, smiling. "It is very much appreciated."

"Yes, thank you," Lisa whispered, smiling, following on behind.

Approaching their mother, not wanting to make her jump, they cautiously walked towards her. Elizabeth had been looking out of the window, seeing their reflections she turned around. Smiling initially, their serious facial expressions made Elizabeth burst into tears. Picking up their pace they both hurried to her, putting their arms around her they hugged her tight.

Elizabeth winced. "Ouch." Gently moving away from them, she pulled her clinging nightie away from her.

Both looking concerned, they stepped backwards. "Oops, so sorry Mum," Susan said.

Collecting two chairs from the corner, Lisa placed them down at the side of Elizabeth's bed, making sure that she did not scrape them along the floor.

Keeping their conversation as quiet as possible, the whispering often becoming louder.

"Mum, what's happened? How are you?" Susan said, scraping her chair along the floor to get closer to Elizabeth. Reaching out she touched Elizabeth's hand.

Her tears had stopped, but the sobbing noises continued. "I've been better. I've been my usual clumsy self and fallen down the stairs."

Seeing how upset her mum was, made Lisa feel annoyed. She just wanted Elizabeth to toughen up and own up to what a bully John was. "Why are you in the burns ward then Mum?" Lisa said. "What really happened?

Cut the bullshit and be honest. I can see the burns on your chest you know."

An elderly lady in the next bed looked over at them, disgusted with the language that was coming out of Lisa's mouth she turned over to turn her back to them. Standing up Lisa pulled the curtain around them for more privacy.

Elizabeth tried her best to hold back the tears. "I spilt a pan of boiling water down myself. I just get clumsier as I get older."

Still frowning, Susan turned around to look at Lisa. "Jesus, back off a bit Lisa. Can't you see Mum's in agony?"

"Back off, are you for real?" Lisa snapped back at Susan. Turning back to Elizabeth she carried on with her grilling. "How on earth did you burn your chest? Were you carrying the pan on your head or something?"

Susan did not answer Lisa back, instead sitting back in her chair she gave out a loud attention-seeking sigh and continued with the frowning. The nurse was now standing at the foot of the bed, a strict expression on her face, staring at Lisa and Susan in turn. "Can you ladies please keep the noise down, you are disturbing my other patients. I am going to have to ask you to leave shortly and ask you to come back tomorrow during the visiting hours, where I hope you will act in a more grown up manner."

With that the nurse left and could be heard talking to the elderly lady in the bed next to them.

Leaning forward Lisa whispered to Elizabeth. "I called in to see Dad before we came to visit you. He made it obvious that he couldn't wait to see the back of me. I haven't seen him for ages and he couldn't even muster up a hello or how are you?" Lisa was angry, feeling like she had been dragged away from her life to have to put up with what she had originally escaped from. "You've got to stop protecting that man, Mum, he's a complete and utter arsehole. He has no soul."

"You don't know it was Dad." Susan had always lived her life with her head in the sand, preferring to hide away from what had so obviously been staring her in the face. "Why do you always have to be so nasty?"

Without turning around to look at Susan and without biting, Lisa remained calm. "Yes it was and you know that as well as me." Lisa moved even closer to Elizabeth, speaking quietly into her ear, "Mum, what have you told the doctors and nurses?"

Lisa's face was close to Elizabeth's, as she watched her mouth movements and looked her straight in the eye. "That I spilt a pan of boiling hot water down myself."

Lisa knew that she was lying. "Do they believe you?"

Elizabeth started to get flustered, tears rolling down her face. "Yes, I think so or they would have called the police, wouldn't they? Please Lisa, I don't want any more trouble."

Sitting back down into her chair, Lisa put her hand on top of Elizabeth's hand and gave it a gentle squeeze. "Mum, please, I'm begging you. Tell me what really happened?"

Susan's frown had disappeared, remaining quiet she knew that there was more to this situation and admitted to herself that she wanted to know the truth too. They both sat there waiting for Elizabeth to respond. Susan was biting her bottom lip in anticipation of what she was about to hear, whilst Lisa remained calm but stared at Elizabeth unwittingly without blinking.

Prompting an answer, Lisa said, "I can't and I won't let this go this time Mum. I need to know now, just tell me."

Elizabeth's hand had started to shake. "What will you do?" The sadness in her eyes could not disguise the fact that she was hiding something.

Lisa did not answer, knowing that Elizabeth would give in first.

Shaking her head, as though trying to stop herself from answering, Elizabeth said, "All right, your father threw the water at me."

Susan began to quietly sob, sniffling she wiped away the tears from her eyes with the back of her hand.

Lisa knew what the answer was going to be but it did not make it feel any easier. "Accidentally or on purpose?"

An escape mechanism had now been released, Elizabeth relieved that the truth was finally coming out after years of mental and physical torment. A weight lifted from her shoulders, her face looked more relaxed. "On purpose. All because we didn't have any spare batteries in the house for his precious television remote. He can never be bothered to just get up from his backside and press the buttons on the damn television itself."

Lisa felt her heart pulsating against her ribcage, standing up she leant forward and kissed Elizabeth on her forehead. "I'm going to go and give Grandma and Grandad Parkins a call. I'm going to ask them to fly over as soon as they can."

Elizabeth smiled, nodding her head in agreement.

Susan remained seated, looking confused. "Why? What can they do?"

Lisa was amazed by Susan's lack of thought, unsure if it was deliberate or if she genuinely was not on the same wavelength as her. "They could take Mum back to Spain with them. Get her away from that monster, even if it's just for a little while."

Appearing to still be naïve, Susan had always protected John. "He's not always like that Lisa." A brash tone to her voice.

Lisa's frown towards Susan should have turned her to stone. "So you think that it's okay for him to scald our mother? Wow, you've got a short and selective memory if you're still putting that man on a pedestal."

"I have to admit he is getting worse though," Elizabeth said, trying to convince Susan. "If I'm being perfectly honest I don't even love him anymore."

"No Mum," Susan said. "It will be okay. Things will calm back down again and get back to how they used to be."

"That's exactly what I don't want," Elizabeth tried to console Susan. "Please don't make this any harder for me. You know deep down what he's really like. You need to come to terms with that just like I finally have. Would you do me a favour?"

"Yes of course I will Mum." Susan appeared only too eager to help.

"Would you go and get me a couple of magazines from the shop please? I just need to have a quick word with Lisa." Elizabeth reached over into the drawer of the cabinet that was next to her bed. Getting out her purse, she took out a five-pound note. "You don't mind do you?"

Holding out her hand, Susan took the note from Elizabeth. "Yes, no worries." Her response did not correspond with what she was thinking.

Elizabeth watched as Susan walked out of sight.

Waving her hand in front of Elizabeth's face, Lisa said. "I'll go and make that phone call now Mum."

Elizabeth held out her hand, managing to grab Lisa by her wrist. "Please wait Lisa."

"Mum, don't try to stop me. Do you know how much I hate what he's done to us all these years?" Her eyes were now filled with tears as she tried to focus through blurred vision. "I hate the way he treats you, like you're his little slave. I don't really care about how he treats me anymore, I'm immune to it." Elizabeth released Lisa's wrist from her grip. "I'm not going to stop you. I just need you to come back tomorrow, I need to tell you something without Susan being about. We don't have time to talk now because Susan could be back anytime."

"Okay Mum, I will. I'll be back soon once I've spoken to Grandma." Standing up Lisa walked out of the ward with her telephone pressed against her ear.

Susan was back at Elizabeth's bedside by the time Lisa had finished on her call, sitting on the chair that Lisa had been sitting on, closer to Elizabeth.

Walking around to the other side of the bed, Lisa leant forward and spoke quietly. "They're going to get a flight tomorrow. I haven't told them everything though. You need to do that Mum." Nodding, Lisa tried to reassure her with a smile too.

"Thanks Lisa."

Lisa had spotted the nurse looking over at them, deciding to leave before she outstayed her welcome. "I'm going to head back to the bed and breakfast now. I'll see you soon."

Looking proudly at Lisa, Elizabeth said. "Oh and congratulations on passing your driving test. You kept that one a bit quiet and I hear that you've bought yourself a car too."

"Thanks Mum." Lisa said. Turning around she winked, giving her a little wave. "We've got a lot of catching up to do."

Driving back to the bed and breakfast, she put on the radio, *Mony Mony* by Billy Idol was blasting out, Lisa could not resist singing her heart out along to it.

The journey seemed shorter on the way back. Parking up she locked up the car and made her way up to her room. It was getting late, taking off her make-up she had a quick body wash before cleaning her teeth.

Emptying the contents of her case, Lisa realised that she had forgotten her pyjamas, which meant that she would either have to sleep in her knickers and a tee-shirt or go naked.

It took her a good while to get to sleep, she'd had plenty going on that day. The distant train sounded comforting as she eventually managed to drift off.

Chapter Nine

The Truth

Lisa awoke the next morning to the sound of the telephone ringing on the dressing room table in the bedroom. Not waking her straight away, it was a more gentle sound than her alarm clock at home. Picking up her watch from the bedside table, she looked at it, it was exactly seven thirty. She had asked reception to give her an alarm call so that she could go down and get her breakfast early. After answering the telephone, she laid back down on the bed for a few moments longer, to try and give herself a little longer to come around. Feeling more tired than usual with a different, weird and nauseous kind of feeling. It was so strange, a feeling that she had not experienced before.

Finally managing to sit up in bed, she got herself up and got dressed. Putting a brush through her hair, she tied it up with a scrunchy, deciding that she would shower after she had eaten. Rubbing her eyes, she got out any bits that had settled in her tear ducts during the night. She was the first guest down for breakfast, which meant that the dining area was peaceful and gave her time to reflect. A welcoming smell greeted her as she entered. The breakfast spread was impressive, all ingredients had been locally sourced. It was a small room with just a few tables set out impressively. The décor was tasteful and looked expensive. Starting with a bowl of grapefruit and a natural yoghurt, she moved onto the more filling food. Not sure when she was going to eat again, she tucked into a full English breakfast, excluding the black pudding. It was delicious and everything had been either grilled or boiled. Before going back up to her room, she had another glass of fresh orange juice, just for good measure.

The floorboards creaked as she walked back up the stairs and along the landing to her room, she could hear faint conversations through the doors from the other guest rooms. Closing her door gently behind her, she picked up the remote control for the television and flicked it on, so that she could catch up with the local news. Whilst getting undressed she heard the tap turn on and off in the bathroom. Walking slowly towards the bathroom door, she opened it, half expecting to see another guest in there. Looking down into the washbasin the last few drops of water were trickling down the plughole. The bathroom was empty but there was a faint aroma, like someone had just passed through smoking a cigar. It was familiar, the exact same smell that she had noticed when she first moved in to her apartment.

Reaching up, Lisa opened the window, locking it on night vent. Feeling for the light switch outside the bathroom door, she turned it on so that it triggered the extraction. Whilst trying to work out how the shower operated she suddenly felt sick again, hurrying toward the toilet she managed to get there in time and vomited. Sitting down on the floor, she felt hot and clammy, kneeling up and holding onto the sides of the toilet she retched and vomited once more. Flushing the toilet, she sat down on the floor again, the breeze from the window making her feel slightly better. Putting her head back, she closed her eyes and waited for the nausea to pass.

Standing up she felt a little weak. Taking her time, Lisa worked out how to use the shower and had the water cooler than usual. Letting the water stream over her face and down over her body, she closed her eyes and breathed calmly. Turning off the shower, she felt refreshed. Wrapping a towel around herself, she went over to the washbasin to put some paste onto her toothbrush. Looking at herself in the heated mirror a scary thought entered her mind, wide eyed and feeling nervous, she could not actually remember the last time she had her period. Usually able to pinpoint it, on this occasion she had lost all track of time.

The telephone started to ring interrupting her line of thought. Spitting any remaining toothpaste into the basin, she wiped her lips on a facecloth before going back through into the bedroom. Putting the television on mute, she answered the phone, unsure of who would be ringing her so early. "Hello," Lisa said, warily.

"Hi Lisa, its Susan. Sorry for ringing you so early. I wasn't sure if you would be up out of bed yet. I just wanted to know what time you were planning on visiting Mum today."

Lisa felt bad that she had to lie to Susan, she hoped that she sounded convincing, telling lies was not one of her strengths and it was made worse by the fact that Susan sounded so sincere. "Morning Susan, no you're fine, I still get up early. You know me, I've never been one for lying in bed. I wasn't going to visit Mum until later today. I've got a few things that I need to do this morning."

A hint of disappointment peeked through in her voice but she maintained it well. "Would it be okay if I tagged along with you again later today? I'm not really a big fan of hospitals and would prefer to go along with somebody else."

Wanting to cut the conversation to a minimum, Lisa wanted to get out of the wet towel and get dressed. "Yes, no worries, I'll give you a ring a bit later on and we'll work something out."

"Okay, thanks, Lisa."

Lisa knew that Susan was smiling at the other end of the line. "See you soon," she responded positively.

Turning the television off, Lisa sat naked on the edge of the bed and finished off drying in between her toes. Standing up she caught sight of her stomach in the dressing table mirror and turned sideways. Exaggerating her breathing, she breathed in and out and convinced herself that her stomach did not look bigger. Putting her hand onto her belly, as though she had some sort of psychic ability and was able to feel if she was pregnant or not, she shook her head and laughed at herself. Getting dressed however, she noticed that her jeans were feeling a little bit tighter.

Checking to make sure that she had turned everything off she put on her trainers and jacket. Grabbing her bag and car keys, she left the room to make her way to the hospital.

The traffic was a nightmare, feeling like she was in a real life hazard and perception test. Panicked mums parking in the wrong places and causing obstructions, parents and their children running about trying to get to school on time and people making their way to work. Lisa stopped at every zebra crossing and each set of traffic lights was against her. Eventually reaching her destination, she arrived in time for the first visiting hours, parking on the same side road again. Walking along the road and into the hospital, she stopped in at the shop, buying Elizabeth a bunch of red carnations and a box of chocolates.

Lisa was surprised to see that Grandma and Grandad Parkins had already arrived from Spain and were sitting at Elizabeth's bedside.

"Hi, Grandma. Hi, Grandad. My God how long has it been since I last saw you?" Lisa said, surprisingly. "You managed to get here quickly." In turn, she hugged her grandma and grandad, kissing each of them on the cheek before gently hugging Elizabeth and pecking her on the forehead.

"Yes, we decided to get a flight as soon as we could, we were so worried. Your mum has told us what has happened and to be honest it doesn't really come as a shock to us." Grandma Parkins looked at Lisa giving her a smile. "My, Lisa, I have to say that you are positively glowing? Have you got something you need to tell us?"

Lisa gave out a nervous laugh. "No I don't think so." Feeling herself go slightly red, she got herself another chair and sat at the opposite side of the bed from her grandparents.

A friendly faced nurse walked over to them, her bedside manner was much warmer than the nurse from the previous night. "Only two to a bedside I'm afraid, hospital regulations."

Grandad stood up, losing his balance slightly he grabbed at the back of the chair. "I'll go and see if I can find a vase for those beautiful flowers and stretch my legs at the same time. I'll leave you three beautiful ladies to have a good catch up."

"Thank you Grandad." Lisa watched as he shuffled, more than walked, out of the room. Turning to look at Elizabeth before reaching out to hold her hand, she said. "And how are you feeling today Mum?"

Elizabeth looked happier in herself, more than she had done the night before, in fact Lisa could not remember the last time she saw her looking so cheerful. "I'm okay in myself. I'm still a bit sore though, which obviously goes without saying."

Letting go of Elizabeth's hand, Lisa walked around to the other side of the bed, crouching down she leant forward. Putting her arms around her grandma, she gave her a gentle hug. A mixed smell of mothballs and a musky perfume greeted her. "How are you and Grandad? I've missed you both."

Putting her hand onto Lisa's back, Grandma Parkins said. "We're fine Lisa, not getting any younger though. Anyway go and sit yourself down, your mum needs to talk to you about something."

Sitting back down Lisa looked at Elizabeth. "What is it?" Lisa looked concerned, her eyes filled with tears. "Oh my God Mum, you're not dying are you?"

Propping her pillows up behind her, Elizabeth sat up making herself comfortable. Leaning forward a serious expression replaced her cheerfulness. "I need you to listen to me carefully and I need you to understand. I don't want you to get upset or angry or make a scene."

"Okay Mum, I'll try. I'm all ears," Lisa said jokingly, trying to calm the serious atmosphere.

"I'm telling you now whilst I can because John's not here and while I have the courage. I needed you to be here, so that I could look you in the eyes when I told you. I didn't want to explain over the telephone."

Grandma Parkins got up from her chair and went to stand behind Lisa, putting her hands on Lisa's shoulders she kissed her on the top of her head.

"I'm so very sorry, Lisa. I do realise that I should have told you years ago. I didn't know how and I was just too scared to." Elizabeth looked up at her mother, taking a deep breath she gulped before continuing. Grandma Parkins nodded her head encouraging Elizabeth to carry on. "I'm going to come straight to the point and tell you outright, John isn't your real father. Your real father was one of John's friends. He's your biological father or should I say, was. You look so much like him and I know he would have been so proud of you. You remind me so much of him."

Lisa remained quiet, intrigued, she continued to listen to Elizabeth. She knew that she should have felt shocked but the truth was she didn't. Always knowing that something was not quite right with her life, it all started to make sense.

Elizabeth spoke more quietly, the old lady in the bed next to them could have been pretending to be asleep. "I met him through John and started to see him at the same time. It was only ever supposed to be a bit of fun. I didn't think it would turn in to anything serious. John and I had only really just started seeing each other. Everything happened so fast. John was so intense and serious and Peter Hurst was such a loveable rogue and had all the qualities that John didn't. I just wish that I had met him first. Oh how I loved him." Talking about him made Elizabeth smile and she looked genuinely happy. "When I was a few weeks pregnant I was going to finish things with John when suddenly, like a bolt out of the blue, Peter died. John told me that he was shot and died in a bank raid. I never saw him again. I was heartbroken and I just couldn't imagine being a single mum. I didn't want to be, so I decided the easiest thing to do would be to stay with John. I really didn't have much choice. I hope you understand, Lisa."

"Peter, my real dad, died in a bank raid? Was he robbing the bank or was he an innocent bystander?" Lisa was not really bothered which way that answer was going to go, a relieved feeling had come over her and she fully understood why it had been difficult for Elizabeth to tell her.

"Unfortunately he was one of the bank robbers. Strangely he'd never mentioned anything to me about that side of his profession. I thought we knew everything about each other. So, as you can imagine, that came as quite a shock to me. Lisa, you have to understand that Peter was a very caring man who would have gone to any lengths to help the ones that he loved."

Grandad Parkins had returned, he looked and knew what the topic of conversation had been. "One of the nurses will bring a vase for you, when they manage to find a spare one," he interrupted.

"I'll go and stretch my legs now. Are you going to be okay Lisa?" Grandma Parkins said.

Lisa was deep in thought and did not respond. Grandad flopped down onto the chair and gave out a tired sigh. Elizabeth waited for Lisa's inevitable questioning.

"How do you know Peter was my father and not John?"

"Because I hadn't slept with John. When you were born I told John that you were premature."

"Did John know about you and my real dad? Did he know he wasn't really my father? Did he know that his friend was my father?"

"No, I don't think so. To be honest we never really talked about it," Elizabeth said, the relief on her face was evident, to get that off her chest after so many years.

"Did Dad know about me?"

"Yes he did. He was so excited. We had started to make plans together, which is why I was so surprised when John told me that he had been killed in that bank raid." Lisa felt mixed emotions, sadness for her real father and never meeting him and anger towards the man who had bullied and undermined her all her life.

"I just wish you had told me long before now." Lisa looked a little disappointed. "Mum, did Peter smoke cigars?"

"Yes he did. Why do you ask?" Elizabeth looked surprised.

"Oh just a feeling. Do you have any photographs of him or any newspaper cuttings about when he robbed that bank? I want to know more about him. I want to know everything about him."

"Funny thing is Lisa; I never saw anything in the newspapers about it. I looked for days after but there was no mention of it. I think I've still got a photo of him hidden away somewhere. I'll hunt it out when I get a chance. I'll let you have it." Elizabeth winked, she was so pleased that Lisa had taken the news so well.

"What are you doing here? I thought you were going to ring me?" Susan's expression was one of disappointment.

Lisa turned around; Susan was standing right behind her. "Hi Susan, I was just passing so I thought I would pop in."

Taking off her jacket Susan put it on the back of Lisa's chair. "What have I missed?" Susan looked around.

"Nothing much really. I'm going to have to get off now." Lisa had gone pale, her complexion looked clammy. "I'm not feeling too well and I've got a few things that I need to do."

"Will I see you soon?" Elizabeth looked concerned.

"Of course, now take care." Lisa put her hands on Elizabeth's shoulders and kissed her on the cheek. "I'll come back tonight. See you soon Grandad, give Grandma my love and Susan, I'll ring you later today."

Chapter Ten

John and Elizabeth

John Parkins and Elizabeth Buckley were still in the early stages of their relationship, only meeting a few months earlier. John would take the long journey and travel up from Cornwall to visit Elizabeth whenever he got the chance, usually straight after finishing work on the Friday so that he could make the most of his weekend. He would eventually visit every weekend. The train fares were not cheap and it would take up quite a lot of his hard-earned cash. Arriving kitted out with his rucksack he would pitch his tent in the corner of the field in Beechwood Park. After a few times other local lads saw an opportunity and would do the same, nobody ever bothered them or complained.

They loved being in the park together without the prying eyes of their parents. Elizabeth would sneak away to meet him there, telling her parents that she was going to meet her friends and would be back late. They would smile, they too had been young once, remembering what it was like to be free without a care in the world and your life in front of you. Too much perfume and extra effort with make-up and her wardrobe were the giveaway. Each generation doing the same things and convincing themselves that they were the first ones to do it.

Sitting at the side of the river, they would share a picnic and look up at the stars together. John would talk about what had happened to him that week at work and Elizabeth would listen, well sometimes. Letting her mind wander, she would daydream about meeting a tall handsome stranger who would sweep her off her feet and look after her forever as though she were a princess. John made her feel comfortable but she was not sure if he was going to be the one. Enjoying the thrill of sneaking off to meet him made her feel all grown up and that would be all right for the time being.

John sat near the river waiting for Elizabeth. He had been waiting there for some time and had started to feel like he had been stood up; his patience had started to wear thin. Normally quite punctual, she was running behind schedule that particular evening. A distinguished looking gentleman, smoking a cigar, was walking along the towpath towards the bench underneath the sycamore tree. John caught sight of him, he had noticed him there before, sometimes alone, sometimes with others. Sitting down, the gentleman looked like he had sat on that bench many times before, confident in both himself and his surroundings. Resting one leg over the other knee, he noticed that John was looking over in his direction. He put up his hand to wave in acknowledgement, a friendly gesture. John, slightly hesitant and not used to strangers addressing him, responded with a wave and a nod to be polite.

The man gestured John with another hand signal, he wanted him to go over to join him. Unsure at first, John stood up, his bottom had gone numb. Not really being able to give it any thought, he tried but felt like he did not have much choice. Brushing down his trousers with the palm of his hand to remove any bits of grass or insects, he casually walked over towards him.

The man remained seated, making no attempt to stand up. Taking a pull on his cigar, he blew the smoke out and away from John. "Are you all right mate? I've not seen you around here before. You look a little lonely. Are you lost?"

John looked at him and found it strange that he was dressed in a pinstriped suit along with a tie at that time of night. Maybe he had just finished work or he was a member of a gang. "Just visiting," he responded.

The man uncrossed his legs, sitting forward he held out his hand. "I'm Peter, Peter Hurst. Hursty to my very nearest and dearest. And you are?"

Shaking Peter's hand, he said, "John Parkins but most people just call me John."

Not happy with being mocked, Peter held a firm grip of John's hand. "Well John, it's nice to meet you. You're obviously not local to these parts, your accent is a big giveaway. Anyway, what do you think of our park?"

A strange energy force could be felt leaving Peter's hand as he released his grip on John. Pulling his hand away John shook his hand about, dismissing it as an electric shock. "It's okay, yes. It seems to be very popular with the locals and it always seems busy." John looked at Peter suspiciously, unsure as to what he actually wanted with him.

Taking another drag of his cigar, Peter closed his eyes and inhaled deeply. "John would you like to join us or are you waiting for someone in particular?" The smoke seeped out from his mouth and nose has he spoke, his serious demeanour never failing him.

Feeling obliged, his response was quick however. "Thanks but I'm waiting for my girlfriend."

With a quick gentlemanly nod of his head, he leant back again and re-crossed his legs. "No worries, anytime John."

Looking away John noticed that Elizabeth had finally decided to join him. "This is Elizabeth now." His face lit up as he pointed towards her.

Walking along the towpath towards them, she kicked her feet as she walked, slowly taking in her surroundings without a care in the world, staring up to the sky and watching any birds as they flew from tree to tree. John walked towards her to meet her, trying to get her attention by giving her a little wave.

Instead of greeting her with a hug or kiss, he grabbed her hand and pulled her to hurry her along. "Elizabeth where have you been? You're late for goodness sake."

Frowning, she had not seen John react like that before and it made her feel anxious, it was not a side to him that she liked or wished to see. "I'm sorry, all right. I had things to do and I didn't realise the time."

His excitable arrogance continued as he acted like a schoolboy. "Anyway, never mind your excuses. Come and say hello to Peter."

Yanking her hand away from his grip, she was in two minds if to turn around and just go straight back home. Snapping back at him, she said. "Who's Peter?"

Remaining seated, Peter watched as John and Elizabeth approached him. Elizabeth's facial expression changing, the closer to Peter that she got. She had never even spoken to him before but she felt strangely drawn to him, he mesmerised her.

"Peter, this is Elizabeth," John said proudly, as though showing off his award winning dog at Crufts.

"Yes, thank you John. I'd already guessed." Peter stood up throwing his cigar to the ground. Stamping on it to put it out, he blew out any remaining smoke, from his mouth, in the opposite direction. Leaning forward, he kept eye contact and kissed Elizabeth on the back of her hand. "Well hello Elizabeth. It really has made my day, meeting such an attractive young woman."

Elizabeth blushed. "Hi Peter." Trying to look away from him she found it impossible, her eyes were magnetized to him.

John stood back, proud that he had made a new friend, seemingly blind to the fact that Peter was flirting outrageously with his girlfriend.

Still holding her hand, he continued to look into her eyes, as though trying to look beyond and into her soul. "I do believe that I've seen you before Elizabeth. Do you live locally?"

Smiling, her eyes twinkled. "Yes I do. I don't think I recognise you though. I'm sure I'd remember if I'd seen you before."

Without responding he looked away, breaking eye contact Peter pointed towards the bench, inviting them both to sit down. "Why don't you two hang around and meet the rest of the group?"

Elizabeth felt herself coming out of a trance-like state, sitting down exactly in the middle of the bench, she hoped that Peter would sit next to her. Instead Peter and John remained standing.

Continuing his conversation with John, he ignored Elizabeth. "We usually meet up a lot later but George has to get home to look after his daughter, Vicky, tonight. She's a beautiful young thing with blonde hair and big blue eyes. She is certainly going to break some hearts one day."

"What do you talk about and do you meet up every day? Is there a reason why you meet up down here?" John was curious and had so many questions. "Are there many of you?"

"We try to meet every day. Not always possible though. We meet down here for the same reasons as you two do probably, people mind their own business and let you do your own thing. There aren't many of us yet. There's me, my old man, Fred, and George Willis. Are you two going to hang around then?"

Neither of them answered. Elizabeth was waiting for John to answer whilst John shrugged his shoulders, he was unsure.

"This is George coming now. He's a handsome chap isn't he?" Peter laughed. "His daughter clearly gets her looks from her mother."

Elizabeth gave out a little chuckle whilst John remained focused and serious.

George was carrying a large black holdall, it looked like it had been used plenty and was starting to fall apart. Putting it down on the ground as carefully as was possible, it was obviously heavy as it hit the ground with a thud. Putting out his hand, he introduced himself, "George Willis."

Appearing more approachable and friendlier than Peter, John put out his hand to return the handshake. "John Parkins and this is my girlfriend, Elizabeth Buckley."

George looked over to Elizabeth and smiled. "Pleased to meet you both. Are you here for the meeting?" He looked surprised as he raised his eyebrows.

"Not sure yet," John said looking over at Elizabeth, who remained quiet.

"Is your old man coming tonight Peter?" George asked.

"He should be, he said he was going to close the shop up early." Peter looked at John and in turn onto Elizabeth. "He owns a junk shop in the village and when I say junk that's exactly what I mean. Still it keeps him happy and out of mischief."

Again, Elizabeth gave out a little chuckle whilst John remained serious.

Looking at his wristwatch George said, "We'll have to make a start. I've got to make tracks soon and get back for Vicky. Elizabeth, John, do you want to join in or just spectate for today?"

"I'll just spectate, thank you," Elizabeth said, deciding to walk over and sit on the swing, in two minds if to go straight home or sit and wait for John.

Frowning at Elizabeth, John was certainly not happy with her decision. "I'll join you."

"Evening all." Fred had arrived. Peter made no introductions. It was evident that it was Peter's father, there were many obvious similarities in mannerisms, let alone they were identical in looks.

George started to empty out the contents of his bag, first pulling out a large object that was covered with a green towel. Unwrapping it, he placed a strange looking demon like statue onto the ground underneath the pentangle of the sycamore tree. A mat was given to each person in order that they could kneel in front of it.

In turn, they kissed the statue and knelt back down onto their mats. John asked no questions and just followed George's lead. He had heard of groups like this before and thought that it would not harm to join in, he was all for a bit of experimentation. Elizabeth sat on the swing and watched on, thinking it all strange, wondering why they were playing little boy's games.

John took his turn, looking back at Elizabeth she gave him no response, returning his look with a blank expression.

George started to chant, Peter and Fred followed his direction. John did not join in straightaway; he did not know how to speak Latin. George looked at John, his face looked odd and the colour had drained and left paleness and sunken cheeks. John felt hypnotised, not in control and started to join in as though able to speak fluently.

Small, black, wispy shadows started to sway about on the ground, dancing around the statue. Elizabeth had long since stopped watching and was now looking at her feet, as she swung higher. A flash of light stopped the performance and caught Elizabeth's attention.

"Well it looks like that's it for today." George collected the mats and packed the statue away in his bag. "They didn't want to come out and play for long."

John stood there for a while longer, trying to process what had just happened. He nodded his head at George and gave him a wave.

Elizabeth watched John as he walked towards her. "What was all that about?"

"If you were that interested you would have joined us. I'm going to come back tomorrow and meet up with them again."

Elizabeth made no response.

The weeks passed, John would visit most weekends and spend more time with the group than with Elizabeth. He eventually decided to move closer and bought a house, a small terraced house, and soon started to landscape the garden. It would be sometime later before Elizabeth would move in with him.

Finding herself visiting Beechwood during the day, she so wanted to bump into Peter, trying different days and times until eventually she managed to time it just right.

Spotting him, she first questioned if she was doing the right thing. It was too late, Peter had already seen her and he waved in her direction.

Walking towards him, she played with her hair, wrapping it around her finger before eventually tucking it behind her ear. Trying to look surprised, she said, "Oh hi, Peter."

"Hi, Elizabeth." Smirking he gave her a little wink. "So glad you remembered my name. I've not seen you for a while. I see John most nights. What are you doing here? You're not by yourself are you?"

"I'm just taking in some fresh air, you know how it is. What about you?"

"Just walking and hoping to bump into you. It looks like it's my lucky day."

Elizabeth felt herself blush. "Bump into me. Why on earth would you want to bump into me?"

"I thought that would have been obvious, Elizabeth." Leaning forward he reached for her hand and kissed it tenderly before making his move and kissing her on the lips. Standing back again, he looked at her, his hand still holding hers. Her eyes still closed and her lips pursed. He watched and waited for her to open her eyes again. Looking at him, she took a deep breath and held his face whilst kissing him in return passionately.

Still managing to remain calm and collected, Peter said. "Wow, I wasn't expecting that. I thought I would get a slap at the very least."

Grabbing his face, she kissed him again. "Meet me tonight, Peter." Still holding his face, smiling and nodding she leant forward to kiss him yet again.

"I'll try. I've got to go to the meeting first."

"Why? That's a really strange meeting you go to."

"Listen, George is my best buddy and he's wanted to set those prayer meetings up for years, for as long as I can remember. I don't want to let him down."

"Why? You do know that it's not normal? They're freaky and bizarre."

"Meet me at the bridge at about nine." Grabbing Elizabeth by her waist, he hugged her and quickly squeezed her bottom cheek.

Walking off in opposite directions, they could not resist turning round and giving each other another quick glance.

Chapter Eleven

The Death of Peter Hurst

It had only been a few weeks into their affair when George had spotted Peter and Elizabeth together. He was out stretching his legs through the park whilst on his lunch break from work. Often he would rush home so that he could walk his dog, Patch, a black Labrador who was still only a puppy and a frisky little character. Spotting them at the side of the river, he stopped close to them but they were oblivious to him and an excitable Patch, only focussed and engrossed in each other. Peter was laid on top of Elizabeth, still fully clothed, passionately kissing her. It was evident that the liaison had been going on for some time; they were very familiar, their hands uncontrollably touching each other. George debated with himself; should he interrupt them by coughing or should he push Peter away from her. Instead, he decided to continue with exercising Patch. Unsure of how he was going to handle the situation, it was all so awkward and not a position he would have wished upon himself.

The usual members attended the meeting that same evening, each turning up at their usual times, in the exact same order. George noticed that Peter had more of a spring in his step and realised that he had done for a while, now he knew the reason why.

Whilst kneeling to pray, John looked over at George, noticing that he was a little more distant and seemed unusually uninterested. He kept breaking off from his chanting like he had something more pressing on his mind. George kept looking over at Peter, staring at him whilst in a trance. Even outdoors, the tension could have been cut with a knife, the fresh air not diluting it at all. John had become a close friend to George, they had been through similar experiences in their lives and had both joined a local pub's darts team, a pastime that they both enjoyed. Knowing that Peter and George went back a long way, John said nothing, deciding it was for the best that he kept out of it.

Peter left the meeting first, walking off without saying a word in the direction of the bridge. Intrigued, George stood on the towpath and watched him as he walked away. John had not noticed, he was busy chatting away to Fred. Elizabeth could be seen at the far end of the bridge waiting for Peter. Like an excited little girl, she jumped up and down, putting her arms out in front of her as Peter approached. George turned around to look at John, checking to make sure that he had not witnessed their embrace.

Feeling let down by Peter, he slowly tidied the statue and the mats away into his holdall. Standing up, he placed it over his shoulder. Managing to hide his disappointment, he put his other arm around John's shoulders and said, "Come on mate, let's go to the pub and throw a few darts." Whilst leading John away, in the opposite direction, he put up his hand to wave. "See you tomorrow, Fred."

Like a spare part, Fred looked around and realised that he was left standing there by himself. He did enjoy the meetings which got him out of the house and meeting people at his shop kept him busy during the day but the nights were often long and very lonely.

Elizabeth had fallen head over heels in love with Peter and he felt the same way too. Sitting at the water's edge he slipped his hand up and inside the back of her blouse, spelling out 'I love you' gently along the surface of her skin on her back, with his fingertip. Giggling, she fidgeted, it tickled. The excitement caused butterflies in her stomach and a lightheaded sensation. Still giggling she whispered those three words back to him.

Peter held her chin within his hand, holding up her face he looked seriously into her eyes. Pretending that he had not heard her he broke into a smile. "Pardon?"

Smiling, she nervously chuckled, "I said, I love you."

Laying down in each other's arms, they hugged each other close.

A few moments had passed, Elizabeth felt relaxed, thinking that the timing was right she looked up at him. She had pressing news and was bursting to tell him. "Peter."

Opening his eyes, at first blurry, he looked at her. "Yes, Elizabeth."

"Could you sit up please? I need to tell you something." She did not feel right laying down to tell him such life changing news.

Without being asked twice, he sat upright before pulling on Elizabeth's arm to help her up. Brushing her hair away from her face with his fingertips he said, "What is it? You look so serious."

Holding his hand, she started to look nervous, unsure as to how he was going to take it. A little fake cough and a deep breath before she blurted it out, "I'm pregnant. We're going to have a baby."

Putting his finger in his ear he wiggled it about, unsure if he had heard her correctly. "Say that again."

"I'm preg…" Not giving her time to finish he threw his arms around her.

Holding her at arm's length, he nodded his head, as though he was trying to take in the news and wait for her to reconfirm. "Oh my God. I'm going to be a dad." Peter stood up and got down on one knee. "Elizabeth Buckley, will you marry me?"

"Erm." Elizabeth laughed and pretended that she was thinking about it. "Yes of course I'll marry you, but I want a nice big diamond you know."

Still down on one knee, he continued to look at her with devotion in his eyes. "I love you, Mrs Elizabeth Hurst."

Again she chuckled, she liked the sound of that. She had found the man that she wanted to spend the rest of her life with. "I love you too Mr Peter Hurst."

John and George had dropped off at George's house first to leave the holdall before going onto their local pub to have that game of darts.

George got the first round in. Putting their pints down on a side table, they got their darts from out of their pockets. "We need to come up with an idea to recruit more people to our prayer meetings. Any ideas John?"

Picking up the board rubber, John wiped away the previous chalked scores from whoever had played on it last. "I'll put my thinking cap on. I've tried to recruit Elizabeth but she just does not seem interested."

George was the first to throw his darts. "What too busy?" he said, with his left eye closed as he aimed at the board.

Watching as George hit a twenty on his first throw, without warming up, John said. "No, she thinks it's all stupid."

Laughing before throwing his second dart, George said, "Women, eh!" Missing the twenty, it landed in the five.

"Where was Hursty rushing off to? His mind seems to be elsewhere these days," John asked jokingly whilst stood well back behind him. "He's not got a woman has he?"

The third dart missed the board entirely, wedging itself into the cork that the dartboard was mounted on.

George's manner had changed, appearing impatient and shorter tempered. "No idea what he's been up to."

Feeling anxious, John knew that George enjoyed playing darts but he did not usually take it so seriously. "I thought you guys went back a long way."

Collecting his darts George turned to look at John. He looked like he was starting to get a bit hot under the collar. "Only when it suits him. He's definitely up to something and he knows that I would not approve, hence the secrecy."

John was thirsty. Finishing his pint he decided for everybody's sake that he should just drop the subject.

George's mind and heart were no longer on the game. He had hoped that throwing a few arrows would release some of the tension that had been building up inside him. Deciding to call it a night, they agreed to meet up again the night after, as usual. Now convinced that George definitely knew something was not right and was keeping it from him, John chose not to push it, instead deciding to go home.

In two minds as to what to do about the whole Peter and Elizabeth situation, a small part of George would have preferred not to have seen anything and to be kept out of it altogether. Although a greater part wanted to tell John about everything he had witnessed and then give Peter a good kicking to try to knock some sense into him. Going with a friend's woman was a definite no go area.

Peter was first at the meeting the following night. He had made a decision and nothing was going to make him change his mind. It was now common knowledge around the neighbourhood that some strange cult was practicing in the park. Peter wanted out, he no longer wanted to be associated with it or be any part of it. It had been fun while it lasted and a bit of a laugh at first, never questioning George as to how he managed to conjure up the black wispy shadows, not wanting to spoil the illusion.

George looked serious as he approached Peter with the same facial expression as he had the night before.

Knowing that something was wrong, Peter decided to speak first, "Look, George, there's something I need to tell you."

Placing the holdall underneath the sycamore, he continued to walk over in Peter's direction. Standing right in front of him, he said. "I already know."

Looking surprised, Peter said. "You do. I know we go back a long way and all that, it's just that I don't think these meetings are for me any more."

George appeared to be convincing as he put on an act of dismay. "What you're bailing on me? We've got some new recruits starting tonight Hursty. You've let me down mate." Walking back over to his holdall, he started the usual nightly ritual of emptying it out in order of statue followed by prayer mats.

Following, Peter tried to explain himself a little better. "Sorry I've just got other things to worry about now, that's all. We can still meet up and go for a drink now and again."

George was tired of all the nonsense, deciding it was best to tackle it head-on. "What, you mean John's bird, Elizabeth?" Standing back up he stood perfectly still, waiting for Peter's response and judging his facial expression.

The sign of guilt was written all over Peter's face. "What?"

"You heard me," George said with a smug smile on his face. Slowly shaking his head in disgust, he said, "Don't treat me like a fool as well."

Peter was now showing signs of being agitated as he started to scratch his chin nervously. Stepping backwards slightly, he said. "How did you find out about us?"

Keeping his eye contact with Peter initially until he looked around to check that nobody could hear him before responding. "I saw you both together. You weren't exactly being discreet."

Peter gulped, looking worried he said, "Oh shit. Did John see us? I didn't want him to find out like that."

"Not on that occasion, no. And it's a bit late to start agonising over John's feelings, isn't it?"

Relieved that the secret was finally out in the open, Peter appeared desperate to confide in someone, informing George of his news with both fearlessness and excitement. "She's pregnant George. She's having my kid. I'm so excited that I'm going to be a dad."

George sounded convincing whilst his inner thoughts were malicious. "How exciting for you both. Really pleased for you mate."

"You've got to understand that we didn't mean for any of this to happen. It just feels right, like it was meant to be. Just got to tell John now. That's going to be the hard part. Got to be honest with him though. Elizabeth said she would try to break the news gently to him."

George put his hand onto Peter's shoulder, squeezing slightly he left his hand there with a firm grip. "He already suspects that something is going on but he doesn't know what, at least I don't think he does anyway. It might sound better coming from me. Do you want me to break the news gently to him?"

Looking at George, Peter tried to judge him to see if he was being sincere or if he was joking with him. "Would you? Would you really do that for me George? You have no idea how much that would help. Please try to explain that we didn't mean to hurt him."

Letting go of his shoulder, he gave Peter a gentle punch on the top of his arm. "We go back a long way Hursty and besides, what are friends for? You'd do the same for me I'm sure, wouldn't you?"

Peter had been rehearsing all day about how he was going to break the news to George about the meetings and then the news to John about Elizabeth, not quite believing how easy it was all going. Half expecting something to kick off, his gut feelings were still not right about the whole situation. "No hard feelings about the meetings then? You understand?"

"Yeah of course I understand. Go and be with your good lady. Come back down tomorrow and I'll let you know how I got on." George gave him a wink and a head signal indicating for him to be on his way.

Grabbing George, Peter gave him a big man-hug, patting him on his back. "Cheers." Off he went with a spring in his step, feeling like a great weight had been lifted from his shoulders.

George breathed in and out loudly, trying to control his breathing. His chest rose up and down slowly. His lips were pursed, his nostrils flared and his face became redder and redder. He watched as Peter walked away, the anger was hard to control. Peter had disregarded what George believed in, what they had worked so hard to achieve together, mocking it, therefore George knew that it was time to move it up a notch.

George caught sight of John walking towards him, a swagger in his walk as he passed Peter going in the opposite direction. Stopping, John looked at him and said, "Not joining us tonight Hursty?"

Not responding or making eye contact Peter carried on walking, acknowledging John with a wave of his hand. Standing there for a moment longer, he continued to watch Peter, expecting an imminent response. Instead, he quickened his pace. Looking bemused, John shrugged, shook his head and carried on walking along the towpath in the direction of George.

George had started to set things up ready for the night's meeting, his breathing calmer, he had managed to compose himself.

John could sense an atmosphere; he wanted to get to the bottom of it so he started to question George. "Evening. What's wrong with Hursty? He seemed to be in a hurry. He's just walked straight past me, practically ignoring me. Is it something that I have said or done to offend him?"

George stood up, walking over to John he put his hands on his shoulders and gripped them firmly. Looking him in the eyes he said, "He's left our meetings." His face filled quickly with rage again.

John knew that something else had happened. "Oh, why?" He wriggled his shoulders to allow the blood to circulate, George let go.

Shaking his head, he became focussed again as he came out of his trance. "I need to speak to you after the meeting. Okay?"

Not sure if he should be feeling nervous or relieved, he said, "Yes, of course."

John's mind was not really on their meeting that night. He was second-guessing what it was that George wanted to talk to him about. A couple of new recruits had joined, young spotty lads who had nothing better to do on a night. George had his professional head on whilst John just wanted the meeting to be over.

It was just the two of them again, the young lads had left excitedly seemingly pleased to be allowed to be part of something, albeit unusual.

"We're not getting any further than mustering up a few powerless entities John. We need a sacrifice and I know just the thing," George said whilst packing away.

John's eyes widened, he was not expecting that to come from George's mouth. "Sacrifice?" His frown remained.

"Yes, you heard me right. We need a blood sacrifice."

John froze to the spot, trying to work out if his surroundings were real or if he was about to wake up at any moment, possibly with a wet bed. Not quite believing or fully understanding what he was hearing he said. "What you mean like a cat or dog or something?"

George laughed, staring at John he said. "No. I mean a human and I know just the individual." Smiling, he was adamant.

The hairs on the back of John's neck stood up. "Not me! Jesus don't say me, please."

"No, Peter Hurst." A consistent stare remained.

"Are you serious or are you just trying to scare the crap out of me? Because I can tell you that it is most definitely working." John gave out a nervous half-hearted laugh.

George leant his head forward, closer to John and said. "He's got more important things to do now so doesn't want any part of our meetings."

John stood there with an overwhelming sense of confusion. "So let me get this straight in my head. You want to sacrifice him, kill him, just because he doesn't want to come to the meetings any more. Do you know how bonkers that sounds?"

George was so matter-of-fact when he said, "Yes, that's exactly it. He said that he's going to come down to the meeting for one last go tomorrow."

"So hopefully we can change his mind rather than sacrifice him then?" John said, confidently nodding his head, hoping that George would be in agreement with him.

"Yes, that's the general idea." George smirked at John knowing that within twenty-four hours, John would see things his way, just as soon as he knew what the truth was.

The following day George rang the two new recruits to let them know that the meeting had been cancelled for that night and would let them know when the next one would be. John was not really in the mood either, he knew that there would be serious confrontation but was more concerned with what might happen to him if he did not go.

George and John arrived in good time, sitting on the bench they waited for Peter who arrived a little after them. Only getting out the statue, George placed it underneath the tree, leaving the prayer mats in his bag.

Peter looked obviously nervous. John could not understand what all the fuss was about and smiled across to him. "Are you okay Hursty?"

Speaking more timidly than usual, Peter said, "I'm okay John. More importantly how are you? You seem to have taken the news better than I thought you would."

Interrupting their conversation, George said, "Right guys, here's a beer each. Get your laughing gear around that." Passing them a bottle each, he switched them at the last second, nearly mixing them up.

Each swigging from their bottles, it was not too long before Peter started to feel light-headed, his limbs felt numb. His legs gave way underneath him, he fell underneath the sycamore tree, unable to move or speak. Starting to froth at the mouth whilst his eyeballs had rolled backwards showing just the whites of his eyes. George had slipped a micky fin into his bottle and he was now totally paralysed from it.

John looked on in horror, he could not quite comprehend what George was doing. None of it made any sense. Pouring what was left of his beer onto the ground he dropped the bottle and grabbed hold of his arm. "George what the hell are you doing? What's really going on here? And what was Hursty talking about? He's talking to me like I'm the one that's going to be mincemeat." Feeling the anger grow inside him, he had finally had enough of being kept in the dark. "I want answers and I want them now."

George's eyes looked somehow different as he pulled John's hand away from his arm. "John. I hope you're ready for this. Not only does Hursty want to leave us but he's going to do it with Elizabeth."

"Elizabeth." John frowned. "What, my Elizabeth?"

Nodding his head, George looked down at Peter and spat on his face before saying. "Yes and if that's not bad enough, she's also expecting his baby."

Making no response, instead John's realisation sinking in, he stood there looking at George and then at Peter in turn. His head began to spin. Who were these men? What had he got involved in? Was George telling him the truth? Surely Peter would never do that to him. Elizabeth had told him that the meetings were foolish but she had seemed more distant of late and made up silly excuses for them not to be together. He quickly came to the conclusion that Peter had deliberately set out to take Elizabeth from him.

Snapping back to reality, he watched as George dragged Peter, grabbing him underneath his arms he propped him up against the tree, underneath the pentangle and next to the statue. Getting a length of rope from his bag, he wound it around the tree, tying Peter to it.

John moved forward, knelt in front of Peter and punched him as hard as he could on his nose. Tears of sorrow poured from Peter's eyes and streamed down his face. He could hear, smell and sense everything that was about to happen before it actually did and could not do anything to stop it.

George took a knife from his bag, passing it to John he nodded his head. Reading his mind John knew what he had to do. Stabbing the knife into Peter's heart, he could feel the softness of his flesh. Pulling it out, he stabbed him repeatedly, again and again, counting out loud initially. The blood poured out of him like a river, flowing onto the ground below, soaking into the visible roots of the tree. The roots pulsated before the lines of the pentangle filled with blood and the tree itself appeared to take on a life of its own.

John was out of control as the anger engulfed his body. Cautiously grabbing John's arm for him to stop, George was ecstatic as he pointed at the statue. Alongside the usual few little shadows stood a tall black shadow, looking down at them and Peter's limp lifeless body.

George fell to his knees, surrendering his whole being, bowing to it, idolising it as though it were some kind of superior being. He looked up at it and watched as it simply vanished, not acknowledging them. George stood up, staring down at the statue, feeling cheated he had not been given a chance to prove his worth.

John was now standing up again, looking down over Peter's body. He started to panic as the realisation that he had just murdered another human being washed over him. The knife was still in his hand and there were sores on his palm where he had gripped it so tight. He had blacked out and could not remember the last few minutes. Rushing behind the tree, he tried to grip its trunk with one hand whilst grabbing his stomach with the other. Lurching his head forward he vomited twice before lifting his head back up and retched again before managing to catch his breath.

Wiping away any residue from his lips with the back of his hand, he proceeded to wipe it onto his trousers.

Using the same knife to cut the rope they managed to drag Peter's body into the bushes without being seen. They had now got the task of trying to work out what they were going to do with him.

John's hands were covered in blood, calmly George lead him down to the river. "I was so angry, George. I must have hit out before I realised what I was doing. I've never killed anyone before, you've got to believe me." Washing his hands in the river, he wept with sadness as his body shook, his adrenaline slowly returning back to a level of normality.

George put his hand onto John's shoulder. Looking over at the statue, he felt more disappointed about the entity from beyond the grave not remaining than he did about the death of his friend Peter. He had been researching about the occult for years and was not certain what would actually happen, feeling cheated he wished more that the entrance to hell had appeared. "Don't worry, we'll find somewhere to bury him. We can't do it down here though, we'll be seen or the animals will dig him up again."

John knew that he could trust George, he had after all been part of it. "Okay."

All too conveniently, he came up with a quick solution. "What about in your back garden?" He had obviously given it much thought and careful planning.

John was feeling sensitive and vulnerable and would have gone along with anything that night. "Okay."

Any outsider looking in would have found it hard to believe that this lifeless body was in actual fact a long-time friend of George's, who showed no signs of distress at all. "Have you got a wheelbarrow and something to cover his body with?" George said calmly.

Feeling weak, John just wanted to run for the hills. "Yes I should have."

Walking away from the river, they headed back towards the bushes. George stood guard. "Fetch them; I'll stay with the body."

It was dark by the time John returned. Needing to find oil for his squeaky wheelbarrow, not wanting to draw any unnecessary attention to himself.

"Everything okay?" John said, looking around for any obvious evidence. George had tidied away the statue into his bag. The patch of blood under the tree had been covered with soil, to any passer-by it looked like an animal had been scavenging.

"Yes. You took longer than I thought, did anybody see you?" George had beads of sweat on his forehead.

John noticed that George appeared a little panicked, not quite as in control. Wandering what had occurred whilst he had been gone, he did not question it, instead he said, "Well yes, but nobody questioned or bothered me."

Firstly checking around him, George pulled Peter's body from out of the bushes by gripping his arms underneath his armpits. "We're going to have to be quick."

John helped by grabbing hold of his ankles.

"After three, one, two, three, lift," George said, gasping for breath.

Throwing him like a dead animal into the wheelbarrow, John said, "Jesus, he weighs a ton." Turning him onto his side, they tried their best to curl him up into a ball before picking up the blanket and putting it over him, making sure that he was totally covered. George uprooted some plants and bushes, balancing them on top of the blanket. Hopefully, if they were spotted it would just look like they were just doing a spot of pilfering.

It was not far, luckily they had not been seen. The wheelbarrow struggled and only just made the distance. Taking it in turns they started to dig Peter's grave in John's back garden, where his lawn would later be. There was no light except that of the moon and a few nearby streetlights. George would rest on John's living room floor that night. Neither of them saying another word.

George awoke early the next morning, leaving John's house he closed the front door gently behind him. John heard him leave, he had not slept a wink. He was convinced that either Peter would walk into his room or there would be the police knocking on the front door. Neither had happened which seemed to disturb him more.

Not quite feeling right, George walked down to the scene of the crime before making his way home. He needed to get cleaned up before heading off to work. It had only just occurred to him that he would no longer see his long-time friend Peter. Walking to the tree, he put down his bag and looked at the mound of soil. Taking a deep breath, he followed the trail where the grass had been flattened. Looking into the bushes, he saw a brown wallet laying in the middle. Upon opening it he found that it was Peter's. There were a couple of bankcards in and several notes. Taking out the notes and putting them into his pocket, he tossed the wallet along with the cards into the river.

The hairs on the back of his neck stood up followed closely by the hairs on his arms. Not daring to turn around, he could feel an angry force. The black shadow stood behind him, it grew taller and wider, eventually enveloping George. Unable to breathe, he was flying through the air, stopping underneath a thick strong branch of the sycamore tree. A tree swing rope started to coil itself around George's neck. Feeling the rope getting a firmer grip on his neck, his eyes widened, as he knew what was coming next. The entity stood underneath the tree, appearing to look up. Unable to make a noise, George tried to loosen its grip from around his neck, swinging his body and kicking his legs, he tried to weaken the branch. A python appeared to come from nowhere and slithered along the branch, head first, it hissed in George's face as he looked upwards. His attempts at loosening the rope were stopped as he waved his hands upwards to scare away the snake. The snapping of his neck and the flinching of his body frightened away the birds in the nearby trees. The snake could no longer be seen, vanishing along with George's bag.

His body was left hanging there for an hour before it was discovered by a young lady who was out for her morning jog.

Fred had been ill for several days and had heard through the grapevine about George's suicide. He had taken to his bed with a bout of flu, muscles ached in his body that he had long ago forgotten about. His thoughts were more for his son, deeply concerned about Peter, he had been trying to contact him for a couple of days.

It was not until a few days later when Peter appeared to Fred. Working as usual in his shop, a voice could be heard coming from the stock room.

"Dad."

Fred looked up from his newspaper. A smile appearing on his face. "Peter."

Fred locked up the front door of the shop. Walking into the stockroom, he looked around. "Peter?" There was no sign of him and nowhere for him to hide.

"Dad, I'm so sorry. I never got the chance to say goodbye."

His smile was replaced with a solemn expression. "Goodbye? Peter why can't I see you?" Looking into each corner, even near the ceiling he still could not see him.

"Please look out for Elizabeth, she's having your grandchild."

"What's going on Peter? They found George hanging from a tree in Beechwood. I'm scared." Fred felt an overwhelming feeling of love and could smell Peter's aftershave; he knew that he was close to him.

"Please don't be. Everything will be fine, I promise. I love you Dad."

Fred knew he had gone, an overwhelming sense of emptiness and loneliness was surrounding him. "I love you too son," Fred said, putting his hand over his heart.

Elizabeth had not heard from Peter for days, knowing something was wrong he would never have stood her up for no good reason. John was due to meet her that night, arranging to go out for a meal, nowhere too fancy, just the local Indian restaurant.

Elizabeth sat quietly whilst John explained how Peter was not going to be about anymore. Elizabeth held back the tears, John could see her eyes fill, choosing to ignore it. "Would you like to move in with me Elizabeth?"

That was the last question that she expected to come from his lips. Not responding straight away, an uncomfortable silence followed. She had planned to tell

John about Peter and her that evening, instead she had to make a quick decision for the sake of her baby.

Smiling, she looked gratefully at him, "Okay, John, thank you. I would like to move in with you."

She would save her tears for later. Her heart was broken and would take a long time to heal.

Chapter Twelve

Happily Ever After

Needing some long overdue time by herself, Lisa walked along the corridor towards the exit with a smile across her face. Walking past both sad and happy faces she wondered briefly about other people's worries. Her own recent news made her feel like she could take on the world, over the moon with the fact that John was not her real father and that a man named Peter was, an individual she knew nothing about or had even heard of until that day.

Grandma Parkins had finished stretching her legs and was on her way back towards the ward when Lisa bumped into her. The varicose veins, which could easily be seen through her tan stockings, and the frailness on her feet did not let it stop her. Standing to the side of Lisa, she leant backwards slightly whilst rubbing her lower back. Pursing her lips, she winced and said. "Are you okay Lisa, my dearest?"

Giving her grandma a sympathetic smile, Lisa said, "That news was a bit of a surprise, but to be honest I've had my suspicions that something wasn't right since I can remember. I knew that I was different somehow. A lot of things now make sense and fall into place and I am made of strong stuff you know." Gently putting her hand onto her grandma's arm, her eyes expressed concern for her health. "Are you okay Grandma?"

Giving out a little chuckle, she tried to divert any unnecessary attention by attempting a little humour. "Just a bit of old age and a lot of poverty, my dear." Quickly changing the subject, she said, "Are you leaving us already?"

Hugging her grandma, her familiar smell triggered thoughts about the cuddles that they used to have. "I am, yes. It was really lovely to see you, just a shame that it wasn't under better circumstances. I'm sure that I'll see you again soon though. I've got a few things that I need to do and I'm wanting to go and visit a few of my old haunts."

"Take care of yourself Lisa. Thank you for ringing me and your grandad and confirming what we had always suspected." Holding Lisa's hand, she kissed the back of it. Squeezing it tight, she was in no hurry to let it go. "Are you sure that you're okay? You look a little peaky."

"Honestly Grandma, I'll be fine. Just a bit of nausea, I'm sure it'll pass. It was probably something that I ate for my breakfast." Smiling, she returned a kiss on the back of her hand. "Let's not leave it as long next time though!"

"I always used to have a bit of milk and a plain biscuit when I felt nauseous," she said, winking. "Anyway bye bye love, keep in touch and please don't be a stranger."

Lisa continued walking towards the exit, looking behind her and over her shoulder, Grandma stood watching. Lisa returned the wave as she carried on walking, smiling she was gone.

A pharmacy was just around the corner from the hospital, its dazzling light shone through the glass-fronted building whilst she made tracks back to the car. Stopping, she looked through the window, undecided if she should go in. Her late period could simply be stress related and the sickness could have been over indulgence at breakfast or just a change in the water.

Deciding to leave it a little longer, certain that her body would calm down again, she headed in the direction of her car. The nausea did eventually pass, feeling drained she decided on a little lay down as soon as she got back to the bed and breakfast. A bit of relaxation was needed before she would venture out. Turning on the radio, she sat on the edge of her bed and looked carefully at herself in the mirror. Turning her head slowly to the left and then to the right it was obvious, now that she knew, that she looked nothing like John. She imagined what Peter would have looked like and hoped that Elizabeth would be able to find a photograph of him. Hopefully, it would be small enough that she could carry it about in her purse.

Lying down on the bed, her head sunk into the pillow as she started to doze off to the sounds of Spandau Ballet on the radio. After what felt like a short snooze, it was the sound of the neighbours that woke her with their headboard rhythmically banging against her wall. Chuckling she decided that she would run herself a bath and have a nice long soak with lots of bubbles. Surely the man had not fallen for the sound of her fake orgasm.

After leaving the door between the bathroom and the bedroom slightly ajar, Lisa caught sight of a bright white flashing light out of the corner of her eye. It was coming from the bedroom. Turning the hot water tap off, the steam had started to fill the room, she cautiously walked back into the bedroom. Looking around at the television, the picture flickered. Thinking that she must have leant against the remote by accident whilst laid on the bed, she tried to find it. Looking on top of the duvet, under the duvet and pillows and eventually around the floor, she discovered that the remote was still laid to the side of the television, untouched. The radio had somehow already been switched off. Reaching for the remote she was stopped in her tracks, the scene on the television looked all too familiar, it was her old family home. Sitting on the edge of the bed she watched the screen with intrigue.

Sitting in his usual chair, John was watching the television, his feet resting on top of the coffee table, his big toe on his left foot poking through a hole in his sock. The room looked foggy. John's ashtray was overflowing and a stubby cigarette still remained lit on the top burning through the other filters. In the process of lighting yet another cigarette he started to cough harshly whilst inhaling. His face reddened, a vein on the side of his temple stood out and a blob of phlegm left his mouth, landing on the carpet at the other side of the room. He looked so lonely and yet so pathetic at the same time. Small black wispy shadows could be seen coming through the kitchen door and hovering for a short time until they were joined by the black shadow. Purposely standing in front of John, it blurred his line of sight. Unfazed by what he was seeing, John carried on smoking his cigarette, leaning to the side he continued to watch his television. It remained there for a while longer until the television turned itself off along with all other electrical devices in the house. Now distracted, John stood up. The black shadow turned around and drifted through the living room, through the kitchen and straight through the back door.

Reaching behind her Lisa grabbed one of the pillows from the bed and hugged it tight. A snapping sound could be heard as she bit through her thumbnail.

John followed the shadow, stopping in the kitchen, his hand grasped the back door handle. Gradually popping its head back through the door it waited until it heard John gulp loudly, pulling down the handle he stepped outside. The shadow was waiting for him and hovering vertically over the lawn.

John's eyes widened, a sweat bead rolled down over his temple and he could feel his stomach bile rising. "What the... Hursty?"

The scene had changed, Lisa was looking at Beechwood Park. A young John was talking to a man that Lisa did not recognise. There was no longer any sound, it was like watching an old silent movie where the actors mimed. Another man had started to walk along the towpath towards them. Lisa leant forward, moving as close to the television as was possible. Initially not recognising this man but with a strong feeling that she should. As he got closer, she realised who he was, it had to be her real father. He could have been her twin, they were so similar. Feeling excited she reached out her hand towards the television and said, "Dad." Peter turned and looked at Lisa, a loving smile upon his face. Gasping she sat back again.

The man that was stood with a young John was getting three bottles of beer out of his bag, opening them with a bottle opener he popped a couple of pills into one of the bottles. Passing Peter that bottle, Lisa screamed at the television, "No." Not turning this time, her heart sank as she watched him swigging from the bottle. Sobbing gently, her chin quivered as she watched him lose his balance and fall to the ground. Continuing to watch through her tears, she realised that she was watching as a witness to her own father's murder. The whole sequence of events followed.

There had never been any bank robbery, Elizabeth did not know the truth.

Picking up the phone, she tried to ring John. Unsure as to whether the phone was ringing out at the other end, he did not answer. Slamming down the phone she grabbed a tissue and wept some more. The television switched itself off and the radio station resumed.

John had not got to the telephone in time. On hearing it he went straight back into the house, locking the back door behind him, fooling himself with the fact that would keep Peter away. Walking up the stairs, he remained calm even though he felt like he wanted to run. Rummaging through Elizabeth's wardrobe, he found an old shoe box that was hidden away at the back underneath a pile of blankets. Throwing the blankets onto the floor, he tipped the contents of the box onto the bed. Handmade greeting cards that had been given to Elizabeth by her girls laid alongside locks of hair, baby shoes and pieces of ribbon. All sentimental items that held a special place in Elizabeth's heart. An address book had fallen out of the box and inside had been a photograph of Peter. It fell out, facing upwards on top of the bed. The photograph appeared to be staring at John as he picked it up. Tearing it into little pieces, he said, "You're dead, Hursty. You've been dead for years, now go away."

John had long since sensed that he was not alone. Initially standing in the doorway Lisa's father, her guardian angel, the black shadow, stood close by, just to the side of John. Feeling his chest tighten, a gripping sensation, John found it harder and harder to breathe. Trying to move away, he stood back, spluttering and coughing before he spoke, "You deserved to die."

With his back now against the bedroom wall, John choked as the entity put a firm grip around his neck and lifted him off the ground. His face reddened and his bloodshot eyes closed as he continued with the spluttering. Rubbing his neck John continued to cough as the black shadow let go of him and ascended to float above him. Falling to the ground John looked above.

Putting on a front of fearlessness, John's eyes followed but he knew that his days were numbered. "Why now after all these years? What took you so bloody long Peter Hurst?"

Continuing to hover, the black shadow moved closer to John before fading and disappearing. The local news could be heard coming from the television downstairs whilst other electrical equipment had clicked back to life. Breathing out a sigh of relief John believed it to be all over, convinced that if Peter was going to do something then he would have done so long before then.

A sensation of weightlessness could be felt as John's feet left the floor. Flying with force through the air, he hit the bedroom wall at the opposite side of the room hard, his back cracked loudly. Screaming in agony, he hit the floor. The ceiling light shade swayed from side to side.

Tears of pain rolled down from his eyes. "Did you seriously think that I wouldn't find out about you? That I wouldn't do a bit of research on you. I knew then that you were sniffing around after my Elizabeth." He grimaced as the pain became more excruciating. His breathing had become noticeably louder. Still lying on the floor, unable to move John said, "Is that all you've got for me?" A bedside table lamp crashed to the floor, the light bulb smashing to the side of his face.

The black shadow appeared again, floating above John it finally spoke, "I could have made Elizabeth so happy, much happier than your pathetic effort. The only woman I ever genuinely loved and you took her away from me. You messed up big time and now it's my turn to pick up where you left off. It's my turn to look after Elizabeth and Lisa but not before I give you what I should have given you a long time ago."

Again, the black shadow disappeared. It felt calm again, John breathed a sigh of relief. Not able to move his body he scanned the room to make sure that he was alone. The telephone was not in easy reach, he would need to wait until someone came to visit him before he could be moved. Closing his eyes, the pain had become too much, he needed to sleep.

Waking to the sound of laughter, he opened his eyes and a feeling of dread filled his entire body. The black shadow once again hovered over him and was this time reaching into his chest cavity whilst the relentless laughter continued. Unable to grab the black shadow, John still continued to flap his arms around only causing the black shadow to distort. Encasing its hand around John's heart it slowly squeezed until its hand became a clenched fist and John's heart could no longer beat.

John's body was found by Lisa and Susan later that day when they went to collect a few things for Elizabeth. The coroner reported that John had died from a massive heart attack and would not have felt any pain, dying almost instantly. Susan was the only one to shed tears at John's funeral, which was a quiet close family affair, no friends attended.